FATHER'S FAILURE

ANN LOWE

Cover art and designed by Jennifer Elder
danburyelderartanddesign@gmail.com

Interior formatted by Miss Eloquent Edits

To the amazing people in my life
who believed in me
when I said that I would finish this book someday...
...especially my brother, who called me a kiss-ass for the
dedication above...

This one is for you.

Captain Armstrong's voice and knuckles rapping on the passenger side window interrupted her thoughts. She sighed as she lifted her head. She undid her seatbelt with a click and got out of the car.

"Evening, Captain." She shook his hand for official purposes. His hand was smooth, and she noticed his nails were well trimmed as if he had them done within the last couple of days. "Nice mani," she smirked.

He looked down at his fingernails. "Oh yeah. Monica's idea. She didn't think I would go through with it, but I got to tell you, it wasn't half bad."

"Did you get your toes done too? A pretty pink or orange color for the summer?" she teased. He responded with a glare that held no anger as they made their way to the scene.

Angela's humor dropped and her gaze turned cold as she looked ahead of them at the house. "So, they're sure that it's him? I mean, we did expect this coming being June and all but—"

He nodded. "Twenty minutes later, officers arrived. We were notified not long after to drive up and assist the local department because it looks like our case. Since it took us a couple of hours to get here, they should be finishing up processing the scene. That way, we can go in without having to clear everyone out."

They walked together toward the yellow and black tape. She could hear the whispers from multiple uniforms wondering if it's the same guy, hopeful that the answer

1

Angela parked the squad car two doors down from the crime scene and idled in the darkness. She never parked too close to the scene awaiting her, because she needed that moment. That moment before she got out of the car, walked toward the house, and slid beneath the yellow and black tape. Breath filled her nostrils. She held the air in her lungs for thirty seconds before she let it go through her mouth. Her blonde hair pulled a curtain around her face as she placed her forehead on the steering wheel. If she believed in God, she would be praying for the souls of the family destroyed—but, she didn't waste energy on belief and praying. She gave it up years ago when she watched some stranger lower her father's casket into a hole like it didn't matter the most important person in her world was gone forever. Instead, she pictured the upcoming scene in her head. The son in the bedroom. The parents' bodies in the formal dining room. Certain details never change with William. The only surprise being the daughter. She wondered what fresh hell awaited her once she crossed the front threshold.

"Burns!"

would be no. The captain of the local jurisdiction held up the tape so they could crouch underneath.

"Robert, I would say it's good to see you but considering the circumstances I'll just say that I'm glad you both made good time getting here."

The captains shook hands.

"I understand. This is Detective Angela Burns. Burns, this is Captain Archer."

Angela shook his hand before focusing her attention on the front door.

"The officer who was first on scene is over here somewhere," said Captain Archer.

Angela turned her head at the movement as an officer walked up to them from the side of the house and shook both their hands. His pale face revealed just how dark William made it in there.

"I was the first one to arrive on scene. I've never seen anything like this. He—"

Angela held up her hand. "I have to come into the scene clean. No details. If I am here, it is because your captain believes that it's related to my case. If it's him, I already have an idea of what I am about to walk into."

The uniform looked at her like she was the monster who just committed these acts. How could she be so callous? She tilted her head in acknowledgement before she moved past him to the front doorway. She hesitated just a second before she entered. Two years. It's been almost two years since she started walking through front doors much like this

7

one. Despite the persona that she gave to others, it never got easier.

The stairs in the entryway led up to the bedrooms. She pulled out the disposable gloves from her pocket and put them on as she walked the fourteen steps to the second story. The fifth step creaked under her foot. She always checked in the brother's room first. She recognized the son's bedroom by the half open door with the "Enter at Your Own Risk" sign on it that only boys would think to put up. She wondered how old this boy would be. Her gloved hand pushed the door fully open. Band posters filled the walls. The bedroom suite looked like a hand-me-down that the family painted matte black. The bedspread matched the furniture. Based on the bedroom, he had to be a teenager. Her eyes moved toward the son lying on the bed—posed—as if asleep and unaware of the horror of his family's fate that awaited downstairs. She walked over to the boy and examined him. Her eyes memorized his face as she looked down on him. He had to be about fourteen or fifteen. What looked like about a two-inch stab wound exposed on the neck was the only indication of what had occurred. She followed the blood splatter from his neck wound. The boy's clothes and bed spread were painted in it. Consistent with the others. She turned to leave the boy's room and headed back down the stairs. The rest of the family would be in the formal dining room, or living room if the house didn't have a dining room, if it's William and the pattern holds. At the bottom of the stairs, she turned right and walked into the family room.

She found the parents in the formal dining room, just past the family room as she had expected. The killer zip-tied the father's wrists and ankles to the chair at the head of the table. His intestines were spilling out of his tattered shirt. If he's like the others, the killer cut his stomach open while he was still alive. Above and around the gaping wound, she saw more punctures—as if whoever did this stabbed blindly and with rage. The medical examiner will later give a detailed number of how many times he was stabbed post mortem if it could be discerned. If the killer overlapped, the count then becomes harder to determine with high accuracy. The mother sat zip-tied to the chair next to the father on his right. The back of the chair stood high enough that the killer was able to fasten the top portion of her neck, just under the chin—so she sat up straight in the chair. The zip tie wasn't so tight that she would have been unable to breathe. He wasn't interested in cutting off the airway. Just keeping her head up so she couldn't thrash around against him as he cut her. The sleeves of her shirt were rolled up, and her arms revealed overlapping cuts. Each cut appeared to be made with different depths each time. There had to be at least fifteen on each arm. The medical examiner would determine the cause of death, but Angela would bet by the number of cuts and the blood on the rug that she died of blood loss. Angela imagined the mother crying out with each cut as the tears rolled down her face. Her husband screaming and begging William to stop hurting her. There was no doubt in her mind this was William now.

Angela's eyes surveyed the rest of the table. The daughter wasn't seated. She looked under the table and didn't see her lying on the floor. Where was the daughter? Why wasn't she with her parents? Her eyes scanned the living room again in case she missed her when she walked through there earlier. Nothing. Where was she? There was no one around to answer that question so she walked outside and found the uniform who approached her earlier conversing with both captains.

"Where's the daughter?" she questioned. "She's not with the parents at the table, or in the living room."

The officer turned toward her. Angela watched him swallow as if trying to keep the vomit from coming out with his words. "She's uh... she's upstairs."

She turned and walked back into the house and up the stairs again. The girl's bedroom was second on the left. Like her brother's bedroom door, there was a sign that identified whose room it belonged to. The daughter had chosen, like all little girls Angela assumed, a princess crown personalized with her name on it. Kelly. Angela wondered what new and horrific cause of death William would present her with when she walked into the room. She turned the knob and stepped inside.

She fought the urge to immediately shut her eyes at the sight before her. Kelly was hanging from the ceiling fan by her bubblegum pink bedsheet. Her plastic, purple chair placed underneath her feet. Angela noted how her toes just grazed the seat. She imagined that when Kelly was hanging there alive, she stood on her tiptoes trying to get any type of hold so that she could possibly breathe. The chair was just high enough to stop her from suffocating, but not enough to actually breathe freely. Angela's eyes moved from the girl's neck to her arms. A small gasp escaped her mouth. Small pieces of Kelly's arm were missing. She willed herself to move closer. Her fingertips pulled Kelly's left arm closer to her so she could examine the wounds. He had taken his knife and filleted her skin in a couple of places. She slowly put the arm back into place and fell to her knees in front of the girl as if to beg for forgiveness. Angela stared up at Kelly unable to get up. She didn't think her legs would hold her.

Angela shifted her focus to anything but Kelly. She had to pull it together. She had a job to do and she couldn't do that if she couldn't get herself together. Anyone could walk in at any moment and they couldn't see her like this. Her eyes roamed the rest of the bedroom. The room around her was nothing but glittering pink and purple. A table set up for teatime sat in the back corner of the room. A life-size doll house stood positioned under the window next to the bed on the far wall. The inside faced the bed so Kelly could check on the family of dolls before she closed her eyes for the night. Angela squinted her eyes and focused on the doll house exterior facing her. The doll house looked familiar. She pushed herself up to her feet and walked toward the little house. She studied it for a bit before it dawned on her. The parents must have had this house custom made to model the family's own home. She knew what she would find when she looked closer. It was too easy for him not to. She took a deep breath. She walked around until she faced the interior of the house. The dolls were set like the crime scene just as she expected. A letter sat presented in the middle of the table next to the slices of flesh taken from Kelly. She kneeled in front of the dollhouse to get closer so she could read the note but ensured that she didn't touch anything.

You wouldn't want to get bored of our game would you? I have to keep it interesting.

—A

Angela pulled out her phone and snapped a picture of the note, as well as the rest of the killer's re-enactment. She made a mental note to inform the crime scene techs that they needed to process this dollhouse and the note. She got up and walked out of the daughter's room and down the stairs. Captain Armstrong stood outside where she left him still in conversation with Captain Archer and the other uniform. Her captain turned his head to look at her as she walked down the steps. He didn't need her confirmation. The look on her face said it all. When she reached the bottom, the others looked to her captain to see if they would continue working the case or if it would be transferred over to her like the others.

"You were right to call. We'll arrange for the official transfer of files once forensics and everyone is finished. Detective Burns and I would like to reserve some space within your precinct for at least the next few days in order to have everything together and laid out if there is space."

Captain Archer nodded his head in acknowledgement. "Whatever you need."

He looked at his watch before turning toward Angela. "Since it's already after two in the morning and your drive is a few hours, are you planning on coming in later today or will you be coming in tomorrow?"

"I'll be coming in later today. I just won't be there at eight a.m. sharp like I will be the rest of my time with y'all."

Captain Archer nodded his head. "Understandable. Do you have a timeframe so we can make sure that we have everything ready for you?"

"I should be there about nine a.m., sir."

"Not much time for sleep, Detective."

"With all due respect sir, are you going to be able to get any sleep after being here?" She tilted her head as she posed the question.

"No, Detective. I don't suppose any of us are going to get any rest anytime soon." Captain Archer's haggard face moved from meeting her eyes back toward the house before Angela's captain disrupted his thoughts.

"I won't be with her while she's here with y'all. I'll be needed back at my department, but she'll be keeping me informed of the investigation daily. Thank you for calling us and allowing her space to work." Captain Armstrong shook hands with the officer and the local captain.

Angela just nodded toward both men. "Yes, thank you. Also, please advise your forensic team that there is a dollhouse in the daughter's bedroom that needs processing. The killer left a note and the missing pieces from the daughter's arm inside it."

Captain Archer paled as he let out a curse. He ran his hand down his face to compose himself before agreeing that he would ensure the team processed it. Angela's captain nodded his head and led Angela away from the crime scene and back to her car.

When they reached her car, Captain Armstrong gave her hands a quick, gentle squeeze. "We'll talk details later."

"Of course," she agreed. She got into her car and waited until he walked away before allowing the tears to spill down her cheeks. This makes six families in almost two years. Six families murdered for her.

2

Alexander turned the key in the motel's door lock. He wondered to himself, as he did every time he used the key, how this hotel managed to afford changing the locks on these doors so often since they didn't use key cards. He knew this was more of an extended stay, but people still came and went regularly. He kept meaning to ask the front desk clerk every time he paid his monthly bill but something always took away his attention and so he just hadn't asked in the few months he'd stayed in this place. He probably wouldn't by the time he left. It was getting close to that time to move on to the next one anyway.

He'd left the door hanger on the handle stating that he did not want maid service to invite themselves inside while he was gone. He walked inside and sat his book bag on the little table by the only window in the room. He kept the curtains drawn at all times and just turned on the lamp by the bed. It cast enough light over the entire area without being too bright. It was a long night last night, leaving his eyes sensitive. He took two aspirin with the bottle of water on the nightstand and sat down at the table. He did not have time to lie down and relax his tired eyes just yet. Within the hour, the news would be on. He ran his hands over the soft, leather journal. He didn't have the same proclivities as his father. His father preferred the black and white composition notebooks one can find in any school supply aisle. Composition notebooks did nothing for Alexander. Too juvenile. Too much like the kind of journal a fifteen-year-old girl who only wore black and wrote dark poems would use. Flimsy pages with words to be forgotten over time. No, his tastes ran toward the kind of journal that only a man would use. Sturdy, premium quality pages for words capable of longevity. The pen he used always sat to the left of his journal ready to write his tale with the family. He opened up to an empty page and began to re-live the ecstasy.

3

Angela drove the car up to the side of her house. She saw Robert's vehicle already pulled into the parking space that came off the main driveway. How did he beat her here? She shook her head. Probably because the old man drove like a street racer. His wife always joked that it's because of all the car chases over the years. Angela knew better than to actually believe the old man had been involved in any chases, let alone enough to influence his driving. Small-town Georgia life hardly saw any sort of crime, especially crimes ending in high-speed car chases. It's not like they lived in Atlanta. It's more likely his speed comes from late night country road drag races—not that he would ever admit to such youthful indiscretions now. The lights of her home were still off aside from the porch lights, so he must be waiting for her in the basement. She flipped down the driver's sun visor and looked at her face in the mirror. The two-hour drive gave her a decent amount of time to pull herself together, at least enough to face the captain in a professional, detached manner with this new information. She gently pressed on her under eyes with her fingers. Puffy, but not enough that it would necessarily give her away. She could claim exhaustion from the four-hour round trip drive that started just after midnight if he asked. She knew he wouldn't though. He would give her a pass as he always did when she's had to do a walkthrough at one of the crime scenes. He's polite like that. Her head hurt from crying, but it was nothing a good cup of coffee couldn't soothe. She got out of her car and walked inside.

Meow! Her cat Gizmo ran toward her. She picked him up and gave him a little kiss while he rubbed his face against hers. She walked him over to his food bowl in the dining room since he no doubt would soon begin scolding her for feeding him late, or early depending on how she looked at it. However, when she went to grab it, she noticed that the food bowl was not only full, but there was a small mountain of treats residing on top. She chuckled to herself as Gizmo hungrily ate up the treats now that he'd shown her just how she should feed him in the future. She rubbed his back for a minute and then walked to the basement. The door was closed. Her captain knew better than to leave it open since she reprimanded him two months prior about doing so. Gizmo has too much fun playing hide and seek behind all of the boxes in her storage room. He never ran into her office where she could actually get him. That would be too simple. He went into the room where it took her hours to finally find the little monster. Well, she didn't so much as find him as she heard him scratching on the basement door demanding to be let out so he could be fed after she had finally given up and yelled at him that if he didn't want to come out, then he could just stay down there for all she cared. But, that's not the point. Thankfully, the captain took her loud demands to heart. She shut the door behind her and descended the steps.

"In here!" he called from the office.

"Was that even a question? Where else would you be?" she teased.

"At home in my bed where I should be getting in a couple of hours before my wife wakes me up with the smell of breakfast."

She walked into the room where he sat behind the desk staring at the white board. Each family's picture hung in order with the details of their deaths, with what William wrote in each underneath. The four-month kill pattern of October, February, and June is evident in the dates.

"I see you went ahead and fed my cat an over-abundance of food and treats while waiting."

"Well, when I opened the door, Gizmo came running toward me and then stopped when he realized that it was just me. The disappointed look on his face crushed me, so I attempted to soothe his disappointment with food and treats."

"It must not have worked since the mountain was still there when I went to his bowl to feed him myself."

He cringed playfully. "Yeah... he pretty much gave me this 'nice try' look and walked away. You would think after all this time he would love me more but he's a one woman cat at heart."

She chuckled for a moment and then turned her attention toward the board. The faces of five different families stared back at her. Their demand for justice sat heavily upon her chest.

"So what happened while you were up in—"

"Kelly," she whispered while still staring at the families' faces one by one.

"Kelly's room." He knew she would start with the other members first. The daughter's death always weighed more heavily on her. She hated that those girls' lives ended as surrogates for her.

Angela took a breath before she answered. She picked up the black dry erase marker and moved to write the latest family's name on the board: Reed. Underneath, she wrote the details of what happened to each family member as she spoke.

"The son was found in his room. He had what appeared to be a two-inch stab wound on the right side of his neck. He positioned the boy's body in a fetal position facing the wall to appear as if he was asleep. William made sure to keep the neck wound exposed and the blood spray all over the bed spread so it was unmistakable that he was dead at first glance. The father and mother were found around the dining room table. Both were tied up in their chairs using zip ties. He placed the father at the head of the table while the mother sat to his right. William cut the father's stomach open and continued to stab the father after the first cut was made. The mother had lacerations down her forearms. I'm sure the medical examiner will determine that she died from blood loss. The daughter—" she paused. She closed her eyes in order to compose herself. She found it difficult to pull her emotions out of their deaths even despite her earlier breakdown on her long drive. These families died. These daughters died like this because of her.

"He put the little girl's pink sheets around her neck and placed the chair under her feet. Based on Kelly's height, the chair allowed her to not strangle but did not lend enough height that she could breathe properly. He took the knife to her flesh and filleted small pieces of her arm to hear her scream."

The order resonated in her mind. The father is always the last to die so he heard her scream. He had to sit there and know that he couldn't help her—no matter how much he fought to get out of that chair. She couldn't imagine the amount of pain the father endured long before William took the knife to his stomach.

"After he completed that task, I imagine he pushed the chair out from under her and she strangled to death. He moved the chair back underneath her after she died. The medical examiner will have to confirm this but I'd be willing to bet that's what occurred. Kelly's parents bought her a custom dollhouse made to look like the family's home. William took advantage of that gift. He placed her skin with his letter on the tiny dining room table. He placed Kelly's dolls within the dollhouse just as they appeared within the actual crime scene."

"What did the letter say?"

She recited the letter to him and sank down in her chair.

"Captain, I know I say this all the time, but we *have* to catch William."

He leaned back in his chair and studied the board again with her.

4

Alexander sat behind the wheel of his 2004 Honda Civic enjoying the anonymity it provided. When people think of killers, they think of white vans or dark sedans like the ones they see on TV or in movies. Nobody thinks twice about a common, silver colored car sitting in the parking lot. He looked out over the park. The concrete walking path wound around a playground area centered squarely in the middle. He imagined its design assisted with housewives chattering away with each other while pretending that they're getting some sort of real exercise. It gave these mothers "adult" time while the children slid down slides and played on monkey bars within eyesight. He surveyed the outskirts of the track. The woods curtained the park. Off the concrete oval were designated running paths leading into the woods. Along with runners, families rode their bikes or walked their dogs down through the wooded areas. He smiled to himself and wondered if he would get lucky today in running across his favorite kind of family. After last night, he normally cooled off, enjoying the media frenzy, but it couldn't hurt to at least *look*, now could it? The media had of course mentioned that the local PD called in Angela to determine whether or not the same killer went after this family like he did with the five others. She had of course found the note that he'd left for her. He was certain that they were keeping that detail under wraps just like they did with the others, aside from one. Carving his message into that little girl's torso made the scene he intended for it to at the time. If those notes got out to the media, it wouldn't be hard for people to put two and two together. The notes basically spelled it out. A little digging—more than it would normally take, considering how powerful and wealthy Angela's grandparents were at the time—would confirm it. Alexander's gaze skimmed across the faces before him. Instead of feeling temporarily sated from last night, he felt an itch for more. He could choose any family next.

He licked his lips. He could close his eyes and just end the life of the first one he saw. It was his private game before he found Angela. Not just families. Anyone that struck his fancy. He didn't have discerning tastes before two years ago. He also didn't want anyone to know it was him prior to now. His skin began tingling with excitement. How many lives had he taken before he decided to hide while Angela seeked? He couldn't remember. He remembered faces and details but stopped counting a long time ago. His thumb rubbed his bottom lip as a short reel flickered in front of his mind's eye. His favorite knife entering different bodies. Each face displayed with shock before pain filled their eyes. Pain sinking into blank stares. He scolded himself for the distraction and turned his attention back to the present.

He pulled out his phone and tapped on the web browser app. Angela's face immediately stared back from the backlit screen. He must stay focused. Angela depended on him. He closed the browser app and opened up his music to turn on his running playlist. He placed the ear buds in his ears and the string melody flooded his senses. He got out of his car and picked out a secluded bench in front of one of the running trails to do his stretches. Today he picked the one to the far right. His gaze lingered on a father and son kicking around a ball on the soccer field. It wasn't soccer season yet, so that part of the field usually remained empty. He saw the father kicking the ball toward his son. How old was the boy? Thirteen? Fourteen? *I wonder if he has a younger sister.* He finished his stretches and began to jog down the walking path. If they hadn't left by the time he finished his run, he would find out if they met his criteria. If they already left, they lived to see another day not knowing just how close they had come to death.

5

Angela dropped her bag on the conference room table and looked around the room. The whiteboard, as Captain Archer promised, stood on the far side of the room facing the door. She saw a file folder on the table, presumably with the family's information in it. Once the captain came in to check on her, as all captains did on the first day, to ensure she was comfortable and ask if she needed anything before advising her that they would be just over there, gesturing to wherever their office was, she would get the number for the medical examiner and introduce herself while trying to get a feel of the timeline for the autopsies. She wondered if this station made decent coffee. Probably not. Most don't. She didn't know why she always wondered, considering she never drank from the precinct coffee pot, but she could never help it crossing her mind when she entered into each new precinct. She had already searched for the nearest coffee shop, which thankfully was two doors down from here. She could run by once she set everything up. Understandably, the cops in each station don't want her around, especially if they have a family, so she stays out of their break rooms and doesn't encroach on their coffee pot. She's never there long enough anyway. A few days tops.

She only stays to interview the neighbors or any potential witnesses, get the results of the autopsies, and make sure there are no loose ends before going back to her station. William ensures that his case is the only case that she ever works on, so she wasn't missing anything while she was here. Anything less than her full attention, and hers alone, would cause him to lose his temper again. Her mind flashed to the words carved into the body of the fourth family's daughter. She jumped when the door opened. A man in plain clothing and a shield hanging from his neck put his bag down on the conference table and put two coffees in a cardboard holder next to his bag.

"Who—" she began.

"I didn't know how you liked your coffee so I just got black with enough room to add any creamer or sugar you may want to yours." He pulled out a white paper bag from his laptop bag. "Here. They tend to go overboard with the handfuls of creamer and sugar packets so anything you don't use we'll put in the break room for the other guys. I take mine black so don't worry about pulling any out for me."

She stared at him.

"Oh, sorry. Tad Wilson." He held out his hand for her to shake.

She shook his hand. "I'm sorry. I'm lost..."

His knuckles tapped on the table as he looked down. His deep blue eyes shifted and then he lifted them to meet hers. "I...uh...I was Nick's partner."

"Nick's partner?"

"Yeah, I'm here to help find his killer."

The confusion didn't leave her face. "Ok...clearly you think I know something that I don't."

"The family last night was my partner Nick, and his family. He was a detective here at this precinct."

She lowered her eyes and shook her head. "I'm so sorry. I didn't know names aside from the daughter's, and that's only because it was on her bedroom door. I hadn't looked at the file yet, and I walk into crime scenes with no prior knowledge so I can make a decision without bias."

She thought about how her captain didn't make mention of this while they were down in his basement because surely the local captain had told him while they were waiting on Angela to finish her assessment. He was in for another loud conversation once she got ahold of him later. How could he let her walk in here today without telling her that every cop in this place was mourning their friend and fellow officer and his family?

Tad shook his head in understanding.

"But, unfortunately, you can't help me, Officer Wilson."

"Detective," he replied.

"Detective. I'm sorry but you can't help me. Not only due to him being your partner, though you and I both know your connection with him and his family keeps you from the case; but, also because I work this case alone. It's safer for everyone that way."

He didn't answer her. He just sat down and pulled out his laptop. He pushed her the file on the table.

"My captain is aware of my intentions. He knows better than to fight me on this. Frankly, he didn't want to argue even if he could win the fight. Nick was beloved by all the guys here. His wife baked for us all the time. Kelly is...was... nothing but sunshine. She always put a smile on everyone's faces when she visited here. David wanted to be a cop one day just like me and Nick. All the guys around here took turns giving him future advice that would help him be a better cop. They were my godchildren. There is no way I'm not helping you find this bastard." He tapped on the folder with his finger. "So, read the file and then we'll discuss."

She stared at him. "Now wait a minute..."

He sipped his coffee and shook his head. "Nope, read first. And fix up your coffee so I can take the rest of the stuff into the break room. You'll like it. It's the best coffee around here."

Angela glared at him deciding on what she was going to do. His blue eyes held her gaze, daring her. *He was his partner, and who am I to judge a personal connection to the case with my connection to William. Besides, once I get as much information I need while I am here, I'll go back to the office and then it'll just be me again. There is no way they're going to let this guy come back with me to my precinct.*

She sighed deep and picked up the folder. She opened it and read the report inside. Nick and June Reed. June, a homemaker. Nick, a detective with this PD. Children David and Kelly. Ages 14 and 7. She skimmed the officers' reports and crime scene photos within the file. She saw the scene for herself. She didn't need to read the reiterations of what she already saw with her own eyes. What she looked for was any information she didn't know. There didn't seem to be anything new within the file.

"They're still working on processing evidence. The medical examiner should have us the information today. He knew Nick, and he knows that Nick goes to the front of the line. Lane has my personal number so he'll call me once it's finished. Then we can go and talk to him."

"Okay." She turned away and began to pen the family's name and the photographs on the white board. "I'm sorry, you don't have to stay for this part. I can't imagine that seeing these—"

"I already saw everything. I already spent last night—" He cleared his throat. "Seeing these will be worth catching this monster." Steel threaded itself in his deep, timbered voice. "Though, I will add one thing." A folded family photo was placed under an extra magnet. "Just a reminder that they aren't just bodies in crime scene photos. Nick and I would always borrow a photograph of a victim and put it on our board or in our folder to remind ourselves that these just aren't reports. They're people too. It tended to be lucky for us and you could use all the luck you can get."

She glanced over his way. "Thanks?"

He bumped his shoulder with hers. "You're welcome." He crossed his arms and studied the photograph he added to the board. "So, what's your process? So I know how we're going to go about all of this."

"I interview anyone pertinent to case, get the autopsy reports, make sure there are no loose ends, and then I head back to my station."

"Then I'll go to your station once we're done here."

She turned to him. "No. You will go back to your cases and I will complete this case." She watched the muscles in his jaw clench and unclench for a moment before he responded.

"We'll cross that bridge when we get to it. But there is a reason I'm a detective, Detective, and I have never had more motivation to catch someone as I do now."

"I understand how you feel."

"You don't, but continue."

"You're right, I don't. I apologize for misspeaking like that. Like I said, I appreciate any help and any insight you can give into Nick and his family so I can take all this information back with me and I can catch their murderer. If you want to wait until everything is completed here to have the discussion that's fine, but—"

"No buts. You'll see my value."

"It's not about value. It's about safety."

Tad watched her go back to putting his partner's information on the board without responding. She didn't know it now, but she wasn't going to leave him behind. They were his family and he owes it to them, especially Kelly. What he did to Kelly...little Kelly. The miracle baby Nick and June prayed so hard for and worked so hard to bring into this world. Just snuffed out like that. No. No, this detective wasn't going back to her department without him.

Toccata and Fugue in D Minor played in his pocket.

"Please don't tell me that's the medical examiner calling. I can't handle working with a man named Tad who also happens to have the most stereotypical, stupid ringtones."

He smiled at her and answered the phone. *Oh man did he have a smile that would let him get away with murder.* She internally rolled her eyes at herself. *Now I'm saying stupid, stereotypical things. Lord, help me.*

"Lane said that he should be completely finished with his findings by two if we want to come by after lunch. We'll go eat at Mama Diane's restaurant. Lane requested a rib sandwich and I quote, 'the largest piece of pecan pie she will cut me.' Lane only asks for that if it's really bad."

"Doesn't him working on someone he knew qualify in of itself?"

"Last year, his best friend of like thirty-something years died of a heart attack and he ended up on Lane's slab. He managed that one despite his feelings without asking for that. He's a professional and the best there is. But, this food tells me that what he saw was brutal and he needs comfort food."

"That indicates that he will most likely confirm what I already figured he would find. You don't need to go with me to meet with Lane. You don't need to hear that. Just give me directions to the diner and the medical examiner's office and I'll make sure that he gets his order."

"No ma'am. That will not work for me. If I'm going to be effective on this case with you, I need to know everything. And before you open up your mouth about it again, I am on the case with you. Cap cleared me and he's going to clear it with your captain since this portion of loose ends as you call it probably won't last longer than a few days. That's about how long it's taken you in the past based on precinct-to-precinct word of mouth. You get the information and you get the hell out without so much as a goodbye to anyone."

She looked like he slapped her with that last comment. He guessed she wasn't the ice bitch every other cop, especially Benny the uniform on duty last night, described her as. It lasted no more than a few seconds before he watched her demeanor switch, and that cold, stone wall went back up.

"My duty is to catch him, not make friends," she said curtly.

He nodded his comprehension. He wasn't going to push her yet. He and Nick spent so much time talking about this case, and her and their theories that he wanted nothing more than to get all the facts straight from the horse's mouth; but, sometimes the best tactic is to observe and let the questions get answered in their own time. They always do. June taught him that. It's how she handled Nick on the bad days. Tad turned his attention back to the board. Angela put up all the crime scene photos of the closest thing he had to family.

"Do y'all have a copy of the 911 recording yet?"

"911 recording?"

"Yes, William calls in the murders after he commits them. That's one of the reasons I was notified about this."

"I'll get with Becky, she's the supervisor over in dispatch, and get that for you. Is it like the others?"

"I wouldn't know without hearing the recording."

"No, I meant were these murders consistent with his previous ones?"

"If they weren't, I wouldn't be here, Detective."

His eyes narrowed at her. "Obviously. I just mean... were the other crime scenes like this?"

Her eyes lowered again to the ground, and she rubbed her lower lip with her thumb before speaking. "There are certain differences with each scene, but yes. All of the scenes are similar."

"What are the differences? I am aware of rumors, but that's just cop talk. There is what we read in the newspapers, but they're only printing what your captain says during the press conferences. All that was officially brought down from above was his name, a very old picture of him, and a CGI-looking photograph of what he's supposed to look like now." Tad watched Angela's eyes go back to staring at the ground. He'd remember that tell for the future.

"That isn't pertinent at this point. We need to focus on this mur—" she hesitated before correcting. "Your partner and his family. I need to know about them. What were their habits? Was Nick threatened before this? Is there anything missing from their home? I am going to need to get family members' phone numbers so someone can walk through the home with me to determine if anything is missing."

"I can give you all of that information. Like I said, we weren't just partners. He was my best friend and those children were my godchildren. There is family, but they aren't close. They wouldn't know if anything was missing."

"Ok. Let me get out my notepad and we can talk. After that, we'll go by the house since I'm sure y'all haven't released the scene to the next of kin, or whoever was listed as the beneficiary. Then we'll head to lunch and go the medical examiner's office. Please sit. I haven't been able to try the coffee I haven't thanked you for yet. Thank you for bringing me coffee."

"First of all, I'm not sure who gets the house since as far as I know they listed the kids as their beneficiaries. I assume June's cousin maybe or maybe some relative of Nick's. I don't know how it all works. Secondly, you're welcome, Angela. May I call you Angela?"

She thought about it momentarily. "Since we'll be working together for the next couple of days—"

"Until he's caught but go on..."

She cocked an eyebrow, but he saw a shadow of a smile tug at the edges of her lips. "Just for that you can call me Detective or Detective Burns."

There goes that 100 Watt smile again.

6

They parked Tad's car in front of the house. The yellow police tape still hung around the perimeter. An officer stood posted in the driveway. Tad greeted him and signed them in real quick. She wondered how surreal it must feel for the uniform being posted at another dead officer's home while the dead officer's best friend and partner went in to examine the place. The crime scene techs don't clean up crime scenes, so unfortunately for Tad he'll have to witness all the blood left behind firsthand, as opposed to seeing it just in pictures he had examined earlier. But it was a necessary evil, because he could then give her insight on whether anything was missing from the home, or if William had left anything aside from the message in the dollhouse. Angela walked behind Tad up to the front walk of the house. He stopped and stared at the door. Angela stayed silent and let him have his moment to work up the courage. She couldn't imagine the emotions flooding his body. William took everyone close to her away aside from Robert, who couldn't be run off since he's her captain, but at least they were alive. She could miss instead of mourn them, and for that she was grateful. His ragged sigh reached her ears and it tore through her heart, but she couldn't comfort him, regardless of how much she wanted to reach out and do so. No one ever let her comfort them. They always shied away from her touch like the killer's connection to her made it all her fault. *If only they knew how connected they really were.*

"Captain told me not to go in... that I shouldn't see all of what I'm about to walk into. But, despite everything in me not wanting to walk through that door, I have to know. I know you told me and I have seen the pictures on the board, but it's different than knowing. If we're going to be partners in this, I need to know."

She didn't correct him that this "partnership" would only last as long as she was collecting evidence about his partner and his family. That after that, she would be back at her home office where she wasn't the sideshow. Everyone in her department just pretends she doesn't exist anymore for the safety of themselves and their families. He didn't need those words right now. He didn't need any words right now so she continued to wait in silence while Tad gathered up the last of his courage to open the door and step inside. She didn't have to wait long. Just another thirty seconds or so. She told him they would start in the living room and work their way around the house. The children's rooms would be last. She knew he wouldn't be able to stay any longer once he walked into his goddaughter's room and saw for himself the horror of her last few minutes on earth and how he had defiled what was probably her favorite toy in the entire world.

He stepped inside and went to the left of the staircase where the living room flowed into the dining room, where the evidence from Nick and June lay stained on the carpet around the two chairs. He surveyed the room and his eyes stopped at the table. Angela opened up her mouth to tell him that he needs to redirect his focus back to why they were there, but Tad already moved on to the kitchen. He went through the entire downstairs and confirmed that nothing was missing as far as he could tell. Angela already figured that William wouldn't take anything because he hadn't before, but she wanted to be sure. He didn't want her to "get bored" so she didn't want to leave any stone unturned. She stepped in front of him before he reached the bottom step. Angela's hand lightly touched his halted chest. He was surprised to find her hand warm. Her reputation as the ice queen kept coming up short. He looked into her blue eyes and noticed the touch of orange around the pupil. If it were any other time, he would give it a second thought, but right now wasn't the time. He switched his gaze back to the stairs behind her.

"I need you to..." she hesitated. "Look, if you need a minute or need to stop, I get it. Hearing about what happened upstairs and seeing it in pictures are very different from what you're about to experience, and you don't have to go up there and see all that. I understand that you're a cop and you deal with crime scenes all the time—but this is different. We can get someone else. We don't—"

His eyes went back to hers but this time they glared at her. "I told you. There is no one else. Neither were close to their families. They had other friends but I was the one who was over all the time. I practically lived here. I'm the one who sat in David's room and played video games with him because I wanted to spend time with him. I'm the one who played dolls with Kelly and read those feminist princess books to her because June wanted her to remember that women were strong. I'm the one who—" He stopped and clinched his jaw. His nostrils flared with each breath as he forced his emotion down. He spoke again, but it was barely above a whisper. "I am fine. Let's just go so we can go."

She followed him up the stairs and directed him to Nick and June's room. June kept an immaculate home. Angela found it odd that one side of the bed cover was rumbled and not made.

"Yesterday we worked, so Nick came home and napped before dinner. June used to give him shit constantly for not making his side of the bed back up once he got up. It always ended the same way. He would reply that he was just going to get back in it with her in a few hours, so why bother? It's not like the Queen of England was going to drop by and demand to see their room. She would then say that she just might and he would feel mighty bad in that case. He agreed that he would and then he would kiss her. The kids and I would always say EEEEWWWWWWWWW in that oversized way." He closed his eyes and pain etched itself between his brows.

They moved on to David's room. Tad stood at the doorway and surveyed the room.

"Nothing."

"Are you sure? You barely looked in it."

He looked at Angela but didn't answer her before walking past her toward where she found Kelly. He stood in the doorway of her pink and purple room. His stare moved from one side to the other and back again over and over, determined to look at every square inch.

"Based on the crime scene photos and information discussed about the previous families, his focus isn't the son. The boy's murder is quick and efficient versus everyone else's. He wouldn't take the time to take anything from David's room. If he's going to take anything, it's going to be from here in Kelly's room."

Angela couldn't argue with his astute reasoning, so she continued to stand behind him and stay silent. She watched his eyes reach the dollhouse. He made it across the room in what felt like three steps. Too late to stop him.

"What the fuck is this," he demanded once he reached the interior side of the dollhouse.

He examined the doll parents at the table and the doll kids in their respective rooms. She'd forgotten to warn him about the dolls. She just told him about the skin and note, since that's what the crime scene techs focused on when they had photographed and processed the dollhouse. Angela sent up a silent thank you to the universe that the crime scene tech went behind her and took the rest of the scene away. Tad let out another curse.

"Nick gave June this dollhouse while she was still pregnant with Kelly. June had one of her old house growing up, and she wanted her little girl to grow up with those same treasured memories of playing with a custom-made dollhouse. David played with it before Kelly was old enough to. June was always afraid that David would tear something up. I mean, he was a great kid even as a little kid, but he was a still a little boy, you know? Rough and tumble. But he always moved the 'boring girl stuff' out of the way so he could have battles with his army men. Once David got too old for that, Kelly was old enough to take over. Now it's defiled." He spat the word and he turned back to her. "Everyone knows his name but no one can find him because this guy is one of the only few people I'm sure who can somehow live off grid in this day-and-age. He's leaving notes and toying with you like it's some big game of hide and seek. No one can figure out why." He watched her eyes move to the floor with his last sentence. "Nick and I discussed our theories of course." He shook his head. "Seeing this"—he gestured toward the dollhouse with a wave of his hand before raking it through his hair—"seeing this is something else."

She stayed quiet, sure that this effectively ended any intention he had of remaining partnered with her until the end of the case.

Tad looked at her as if reading her mind. "This doesn't mean I want to quit."

They decided to skip lunch and head straight to the medical examiner's office once they picked up his order. Tad insisted that he would never hear the end of it if he didn't bring the autopsy god his offering. The silence for the rest of the car ride was deafening, but she didn't break it with useless words just to make it easier on herself.

Tad snuck a peek over at Angela. She kept her gaze directed on the road in front of her, but he would bet that she wasn't seeing anything. She thought he was processing what happened to his only family. He wasn't though. He was thinking about how this psychopath family annihilator was obsessed with her. He read the note. What did the others say? Cop talk whispered about notes, but the content of the previous notes were kept on lockdown in that precinct. He didn't ask yet. All things in good time. She hadn't accepted his partnership yet, so all he would get is a skirted answer. Right now, her focus was Nick and June and gaining all the information she needed before going back to her office alone. Her fingers twisted a plain band on her right hand. He appreciated her silence. She didn't push him or try to offer any of the empty words everyone gives at funerals. *I'm so sorry for your loss.* How many sorry for losses had she said over this? How many people turned to her with venom in their gaze and asked why this happened? Asking why couldn't she stop it if they knew his identity, knew he remains so focused on her? Tad thought this psycho picked her randomly. He thought back to his conversations with

Nick around the table. He and Nick used to stay up to date on all the news coverage and cop chatter about this killer. *I mean look at her, Nick. He probably thought she was pretty and thought this would get her to notice him in his own sicko way.* Nick never agreed. He agreed that Angela was pretty, never in front of June of course, but he always thought it went deeper than that. June just commented how terrible this was. Her tender heart always bled for those families destroyed and all of it was laid at the blonde-haired detective's feet as far as the public was concerned.

They reached the office and parked in the front underneath the magnolia tree. Tad held the door open for her. Angela mumbled her thanks and then spoke to the receptionist who stated they could head back because he was waiting. Lane greeted them with a smile and handshake. Tad handed him the bag with the sandwich and the pie. The medical examiner inspected it and nodded his head to show approval that the offering met his standards.

"Have I ever given you the wrong order, Lane?" Tad teased.

"You let them skimp out on the rib sauce once," he said as he pulled the contents out of the bag and began to unwrap the sandwich.

"And I obviously will never live it down, will I?"

A small smile tugged at Angela's face as they ribbed one another before she quickly covered it behind a blank expression. She didn't rush them. Lane took a massive bite before turning to the folder on the empty table. Angela guessed Lane put away the family's bodies out of respect for Tad. Even though Lane was used to seeing people he knew on the slab, that didn't mean Tad was.

"So, I copied my findings for you, as requested by Detective Burn's captain. There is a copy for each of you since y'all will be working together. I also will email a copy of the findings to y'all and the captains by end of day." He said after taking a gulp from his water bottle to wash down the bite of sandwich. He twisted the top on before returning it to his lab coat pocket.

Angela shot Tad a knowing look about the "working together" comment, but she didn't correct Lane. Tad answered with his own knowing look.

"Do you want to go over everything with us once you eat? We can look over the stuff in the folder in the meantime." Angela handed Lane a napkin and rubbed the left corner of her mouth to indicate that he had sauce in that same spot before picking up the folder and handing Tad a copy of the report.

"No ma'am. I have a full day and I rarely sit down for lunch anyway. So, if it's all the same to you, I would like to go over everything as I stuff my face. I promise my mama raised a gentleman and I won't talk while I have my mouth full. Plus, how am I going to know I need wipe my face if I'm sitting over there while you're reading?" He winked at her to show he was just teasing at the end. She saw the crinkles around the old man's brown eyes as he smiled at her. While she might bristle at other men who would tease her in this way, there was something about him that reminded her of her grandfather. Maybe it was the white hair and jolly sort of disposition that reminded her of him. His teasing warmed her and she smiled back at him.

"Alrighty. So, if you don't mind, I would like to start with Nick and work up to Kelly." He turned to Tad. "Should I ask—"

"It would offend me if you did, Lane."

Lane nodded solemnly and then continued between bites. "So, Nick's COD was massive hemorrhaging caused by stab wounds to the stomach. Based on my findings, the killer pulled out the intestines and stabbed him multiple times, both perimortem and postmortem. I counted about nine other knife markings aside from the original stab. June's arm showed overlapping cuts that led to her exsanguination COD. Due to the overlapping nature of the wounds, I was unable to get an exact number on the cuts, but my rough estimate is in the report. David was stabbed in the carotid artery. Based on the depth measurement, we're looking at the killer using a four-inch blade."

"Consistent," Angela mumbled to herself.

"Consistent?" Tad questioned.

"Yes. It's the same size as the others we've seen. We believe he's using a hunting knife, probably one that folds up so it's easier to carry around without risk of injury, but that part is just a guess on my end."

Lane pulled out the pie and the fork, but didn't open the container. "Lastly, Kelly..." Lane focused on Angela's face.

"Based on my findings, she was asphyxiated via hanging. Based the marks around her neck and strands in her hair, it was some sort of pink fabric."

Angela confirmed with a nod. "Her bedsheets."

"The marks on her arm were made perimortem. The wounds weren't deep but..."

"Just for torture." Tad spit through gritted teeth.

Lane confirmed the statement.

"One last thing. Does the folder state the order in which they died?" Angela asked.

"Does that really matter?" Tad snarled.

Her eyes met his. He saw her eyes filled with pain while her voice remained distant and cold. "This will finish confirming what I already know, but it is important. William has a pattern to how he does this. If it's too much, you can step outside."

He glared at her in response before turning his attention back to the medical examiner.

"Based on my examines: David, June, Kelly, then Nick."

It was too much for Tad. The door slammed shut behind him as he almost ran outside to get air. Angela flinched— but didn't move. She didn't blame him. She should have just looked in the report and called later if the order in which the family died wasn't in there. Now Tad knew that his partner and best friend watched his wife die in front of him and listened to his daughter scream while he couldn't get to her.

"Don't count him out. Nick and Tad were two of the closest friends and partners I've ever seen in all my years working with law enforcement. Hell, I used to go to Nick's barbecues on the Fourth of July with my wife. This isn't easy for any of us. Everyone loved Nick and June and those kids. He'll take his minute to get himself together and then come back in. He'll deal with the rest later off the clock. Just don't think that Tad can't handle this or that he's going to let this lie, because he ain't. On top of that, Tad is a great detective. You'll see." Lane took a big bite of pie. "Thank the Lord for my wife's pie."

Angela looked at him confused.

"My wife bakes the pies for the diner. She's the one that taught June how to bake all those tasty treats that the boys in blue enjoyed so much at the precinct. Though my wife will tell you that it didn't take much because June was a natural at baking. It was 'in her spirit,' as my wife would say." He took another big bite as he closed his eyes to savor the flavor.

"For the record, I don't count him out, but it doesn't matter. Once I finish up here, I'm headed back to my precinct alone. It's safer that way." She pretended to look over his findings in the report again.

"So, the rumor is true huh?"

"What rumor?" Her eyes leapt up from the page to meet his.

"The medical examiners have a grapevine just like everyone else. This nut job only wants you on the case. According to Rick, he said as much when he carved those words into that little girl's body."

He watched her eyes dart to the table. "I'll take that as a yes."

She didn't get a chance to answer because Tad walked back into room. "Lane, when are you releasing them to the funeral home? I need to go ahead and make the arrangements as soon as possible."

"The funeral home has already been notified. They're coming tomorrow morning to pick them up."

Tad and Angela thanked Lane and Tad told Lane that he would let him know about the visitation and funeral as soon he made the arrangements.

They drove back to the station in silence. Angela packed her things in the conference room and advised Tad she would type up her report and findings at home since she had a long drive. Tad watched her leave before going into Captain Archer's office to confirm that his involvement wouldn't end here. This morning his captain told him before he walked into the conference room that Angela's superior had denied the initial request. Tad told him that he needed to convince her superior because just like he would tell this detective, he wasn't going away. He knocked on the door and opened it once he heard his captain's voice telling him to enter. Inside, he found not only his captain but another man he didn't recognize.

"Ah! Perfect timing Tad. Come in and sit down. This is Captain Armstrong. I was just telling him that you should be in soon to plead your case."

"Plead my case, sir?"

"On why you should stay on my detective's case," replied the other man.

Tad shook Captain Armstrong's hand. "That's easy, sir."

7

They're back. Alexander watched the boy and his father kick the soccer ball back and forth on the field. He put his earbuds in and stretched his foot on the bumper of his car to prepare for his run. Was this their normal routine on the weekend? A little father and son time on the field? Or is the father pushing the son before the season starts so he makes varsity at his local high school? Alexander smiled. *We'll find out soon enough.* They looked about done with their soccer ball reps based on the son's red face and the amount of sweat the father had wiped off his brow in this heat. Alexander continued stretching out his legs for his normal warm up as he waited for them to walk up from the field to their car. He almost chuckled out loud to himself. His radar never failed to find him exactly what he desired.

The father and son reached the expensive SUV that he'd already clocked in the parking lot from to the vinyl sticker on the rear windshield. The stick figure family every household just loves to put on the back of their family vehicles just like this one. *Father, mother, son, and... oh! Would you look at that... a little sister.* He didn't have to fake the smile that crossed his lips as they slowly drove past him. He even did the customary Southern wave as they went by. The dad's wave didn't come off the steering wheel, but he'd added that Southern half smile that comes with answered greetings from strangers. A vanity license plate of course. It confirmed his suspicion that the father pushed his son to practice during the off season. *Winner1*. Easy enough to remember when he snuck onto the DMV website later. For now, he would enjoy his run and contemplate the little sister's fate. He'd skimmed through his father's words recently and had been meaning to try one particular thing. Maybe she would be the lucky little girl.

Oh baby sister, you're going to love this next one. Father put a lot of detail in this one. This was one of the last ones before your mother kicked him out and moved on with the man you called Daddy. This one even came out while he was drugged up on all those medications. How do you feel knowing all the different ways he pictured killing you, I wonder?

8

William pulled off his rubber cleaning gloves with a snap before picking up the ringing telephone in the kitchen. He sat on the barstool next to the wall since his grandmother never bought a cord for it longer than a foot. She always said that he didn't need privacy with his phone calls because he shouldn't be involved in something that the Lord wouldn't approve of. He kept meaning to upgrade, but honestly couldn't find the point. She wasn't listening in anymore anyway. Her body lay in the cold dirt at the cemetery, rotting away next to his grandpa, who thankfully died before William's mother was old enough to disappoint him with her drug use and illegitimate child. Another thing his grandmother repeated throughout his childhood as if it was some sort of prayer. Besides, soon enough, he won't have the house, let alone this antiquated landline he should have disconnected years ago. He heard the man on the other end of the phone ask if William Richards was available.

"Who wants to know?" William replied. He could almost hear his grandmother's tsking at his lack of manners as she rolled over in her grave.

The voice replied that he was with the law office handling William Harris' estate.

William confirmed that he was the indeed the William this man was looking for regarding the estate.

"I hate to tell you this son, but your father passed away a week or so ago. According to his will, he wanted to be cremated, so the funeral home he was taken to already did that, and you can pick up his ashes at any time."

"Sir, I hate to tell *you* this, but the man never had anything to do with me my entire life so the funeral home can do whatever they like with the ashes." He didn't hate telling the guy on the other end that, but growing up in the South taught him that he needed to pretend in order to blend in. "Now, if that's all you called about sir..."

"No sir. There is the matter of the estate. He has a house that passes to you as the closest living relative. He didn't die with debts; but I must warn you that the house isn't much, and you probably won't get much from the sale of it. You can pick up the keys from our office anytime during business hours since there is the matter of your father's things inside the home that need to be dealt with as well."

William pinched his nose. "Fine." He pulled out his cell phone from his pocket. "Give me your address and I'll come by tomorrow morning about nine a.m. if that works for you. Maybe there will be something worth my time in the old man's stuff." William typed the address in his Notes app as the lawyer dictated it to him. The law office wasn't far, just the next town over. "Can I ask you sir how in the world you found me?"

"Your name and this phone number were listed in the will."

William stilled. He knew his grandmother had lived in this house for thirty plus years and that she, never in all those years, had changed her phone number. Maybe his father just took a shot in the dark that she would know where to find him when the time came. Yet, somehow that statement didn't ring true to William. His father had to have figured that his grandmother would kick the bucket before he would. William shrugged. Unless he found something in that home that told him his father kept tabs on him, he'd never know. Not that he should care either way. William thanked the man and advised that he would see him bright and early the next morning.

———

His GPS informed him that he'd arrived at his destination as he turned into the unpaved driveway. He looked at the old, dilapidated roof, the peeling paint, and the trash littering the overgrown lawn. The lawyer hadn't been kidding when he'd said William wouldn't get a lot for this house. He'll be lucky to get $60,000 out of it if the inside looked anything like the outside. It wasn't sitting on much land, so he couldn't make more due to acreage. Thankfully, the house was at least paid off. *The one thing his father did for him.* In the carport sat a silver, four-door car. He wondered if the keys were inside the house. The car itself could bring in a couple grand. He parked his own car behind his father's, and used the key he got from the lawyer to enter the house. Alcohol bottles and burger wrappers littered the living room. An old plasma screen sat against the wall in front of the sofa. The used-up flowered sofa looked like it came out of the 1960s.

"Fuck this," he thought to himself. "I am not going to deal with all of this shit. I'll just fucking sell it as is and whoever buys it can deal with all this trash."

He moved from the living room into one of the two bedrooms. It looked like some sort of office with papers and an old laptop sitting on a desk. He shuffled through the paperwork and found nothing of importance. He grabbed the laptop and its charger. At the very least, he could wipe the hard drive and sell it for one hundred dollars. He moved on to the other bedroom. He determined this was the master bedroom based on the unmade bed and piled up clothes in the corner. A half empty bottle of alcohol sat on the nightstand. Next to the bottle laid an old composition notebook like he had used in school. A stack of them were piled up next to the nightstand. He sat on the bed and opened the book. He pushed the pages closer to his nose. The scribbles were tiny and muddled.

The medication doesn't seem to be working anymore. The dreams are getting worse. They haven't been this bad since Angela was born. Doc needs to adjust dosage.

Angela? Medication? He put down the journal and went to the bathroom. He opened the medicine cabinet above the sink. Two large pill bottles sat at eye level. He inspected the labels: Clozapine 500 mg and Trazodone 100 mg. Xanax as needed. He took out his phone and did a quick Internet search on the medications. *Interesting*... He grabbed the medications and went back into the bedroom. He needed a bag. He looked around the room and found a duffel bag on the top shelf in the closet. He put the laptop, medications, and journals in the bag. He searched the rest of the house and found nothing worth saving aside from the car keys hanging on the hook by the side door leading to the carport. Whoever bought the place next could deal with the dilapidated furniture and plaid Goodwill shirts and all of the alcohol bottles. He locked the door behind him and put the duffel in his car.

He sat down on his couch later that evening and opened up his father's journals. Apparently his father wasn't great about dating each entry in the journals, or even writing in them, since there seemed to be long gaps of time between some entries, and even between each new journal. But a quick thumb-through and observation of the wear and tear of each one gave him the order of the journals. He started with the oldest.

He guessed based on the date that he began journaling sometime in college. He wrote of meeting William's mother Agnes and the drugs they took together. He told her about the horrible dreams that plagued him since he hit puberty. The thoughts that crossed his mind and seemed normal to him even though he knew no one thought this way. How he could see someone walking down the road with crutches and he had the sudden urge to grab the crutch and beat that person over the head with it until he was standing over the bloody body. His foot itched to kick animals that passed him on the street. He once had a pet dog that he kicked down the stairs when he was barely a teen. His mother saw the smile on his face when he saw the dog hit the bottom. She rehomed it the very next day. He never knew where the dog landed up, but he hoped it was okay and he was sorry about doing it.

Agnes loved the violence. She wanted him to hit her and choke her while they had sex. When she got really drunk, she screamed at him, pushed him, and threatened him if he didn't fight back. He called both Agnes and the relationship toxic. He finally ended it after seven months. His grades were hanging by a thread by that point. All of his friends that he had before her were gone, replaced with his drug friends that only wanted to be around him if he had their next score. The dreams were worse than ever. He knew he couldn't keep living this way. After he ended things with Agnes, he flushed any leftover drugs he had in his apartment and quit cold turkey. Two weeks later she was at his door holding a pregnancy test. The next pages were filled with ramblings of questions about how he was going to raise a kid and how could she raise this kid when she was too wrapped up in drugs herself. He told her to abort, but she told him that she was raised with values that couldn't let her murder the innocent baby inside of her. She told him that if he didn't want the baby, then he just needed to stay away. She'd figure it out on her own. So that's what he did. Nowhere in all the pages did it ever say that he regretted the choice. Agnes left him a message on his answering machine after William was born, but he never called her back.

Not two years later, he met sweet little Southern belle Kristen who came from money. One who he could never share his true self with, but one who forced him to pretend to be the kind of man he wanted to be. One who didn't have dreams that needed to be numbed with alcohol each night. His bride never minded the alcohol since he didn't get drunk and act foolishly. In the WASP society, drinking wasn't uncommon as long as you minded your manners while doing so. She became pregnant seven months later, but instead of telling her to abort he proposed. Nine months later, his daughter Angela was born.

William picked up a wallet-sized picture wedged between two pages. It was his father, holding a little blond haired baby in a pink blanket. He ran his thumb over his baby sister's face and wondered why she was so special that she got to have their father and he didn't. It wasn't his fault that his mother was junkie, though mother was a term William used loosely in regards to her. She wasn't around much while he was growing up. His grandmother raised him out of "Christian duty," as she liked to remind him. The last memory he had of his mother—one of the few he had really—was him walking into the kitchen while she rummaged through her mother's purse after crashing on the living room sofa one night when he was about ten years old. He asked her what she was doing. She just smiled at him while holding a wad of cash that his grandmother kept for bingo nights at the church. She reached over and ran the palm of her hand down his cheek, regret and sadness in her eyes. She told him that he looked just like his father and that she loved him. William asked her to stay, but she refused. She kissed his forehead and he never saw her again.

He continued to read the journals long into the night. He learned how his father's deranged thoughts and dreams worsened after Angela was born. The lack of sleep that comes with having a newborn no doubt contributed to his mental instability. He would stand over his daughter's crib and imagine things that would scare him. One day, he picked up a pillow and held it above his crying child. He didn't actually touch her with it, but the action alone shook him to his core. He secretly went to a doctor and a therapist out of town, and got put on psychotropic medication. His change in behavior and secretive demeanor led his wife to believe that he was cheating. She went searching through his office once day while he was out. Later, he opened his drawer to take his medication before he left for home, and they were gone. When he got home, they got into a fight. Kristen told him to leave and that she wanted a divorce. He tried to lie and say that he was just getting help for some anxiety from work, and that he didn't want to worry her since she had enough on her plate with the baby. She threw his journal at him and told him that she found it in his office in the house. She called him sick and depraved. Once he saw the journal at his feet, all the fight in him left. Why should he fight? She had all the leverage. After the divorce, he initially tried to see his daughter. He tried to reason with his ex-wife, stating he was medicated and fine now, but she refused. Two years later, the stepfather and his friend dressed in their cop uniforms came to his office and advised him that he needed to sign away his rights. Not long after that, he found a work-from-home job a few towns over and drank his thoughts away with his medication every night. He didn't always journal. Most of his entries amounted to drunk ramblings when he did. He would see a blonde on the street and he would dream of killing her later. A man would be rude to him and he would fantasize about bashing his brains into the concrete. These thoughts and dreams he needed to write down so that maybe he would stop seeing them.

The next day, William grabbed the laptop he took from the house and opened it. He wondered if he would be able to figure out the password considering he didn't know his father, but he didn't need it. His father kept his laptop unlocked. He opened an Internet window and began to search. He had his baby sister's name, and it was the digital age after all. He ran his finger against his bottom lip, a habit he remembered his mother saying reminded her of his father. A habit his grandmother couldn't break him of no matter how many times she smacked his hand away from his mouth and told him to stop. He smiled to himself. That habit and his looks weren't the only thing he inherited from his father. He fantasized like him, too. In fact, he did a lot more than that. He stared at the screen as a plan began to take shape in his mind.

9

Friends and family filled every pew in the church. Angela looked around for a place to stand against the back wall, but uniformed officers lined every side. Angela picked at an invisible piece of lint on her black dress. She squeezed herself between two tall men dressed in their Sunday best close to the back wall behind the pews. She didn't look them in the eye as she apologized for invading their space. A few officers clocked her presence, but she hoped they didn't recognize her out of uniform. Her blonde hair flowed midway down her back as opposed to her normal, officer-standard tight bun. Her mother always told her how different she looked with her hair down.

A few minutes past the designated time, a preacher stood behind the podium. There was a little variety at each family's funeral, but most followed the same way in terms of bible passages used and sermons said. Some funerals had speeches from loved ones—but most didn't. Because what can you say about a family slain so cruelly and without cause? This was the most packed funeral she'd seen, but she expected that, since the boys in blue always come together for one of their own. She bet officers from other precincts were here today to show their sympathy for the fallen officer and his family. Captain Armstrong didn't come with her today but represented their precinct at last night's viewing. She thanked him for that and was grateful, because she wanted to stay as under the radar as possible.

She looked around to take in all of the different faces. She wouldn't stay long. She would slip through the cracks once she was able to do so undetected. Many believed that she went to these things to scope out William. Sometimes the families' loved ones found her presence comforting, like she could identify and catch him if he showed his face there to further enjoy the torture he inflicted on the families. She couldn't. Her knowledge of his face was the same as everyone else's, just the age-progressed photo created in the lab. Sometimes the loved ones found her presence scary, or it just made them angry. Thankfully, Southern manners usually won out in those cases because she was never openly confronted. Besides, she was always gone before they had the chance to pull her aside later if they became inclined. She did go to the first few victims' funerals initially to scope William out, but that was before she knew the truth. It wasn't about the families. He couldn't care less to attend these funerals and bask in the glory of what he had done. She attended each funeral to silently apologize. To sit and see the pain she caused to these families. To feel the guilt course through her veins with every heartbeat. She bowed her head as the preacher's words rolled over her. As with every apology she silently spoke, she took extra time when apologizing to the daughter. She begged each little girl for forgiveness for enduring such pain and fear when it should have been her. Eventually, it would be Angela in that situation with William. They would finally face off and he would try to cause her more pain than any of these girls had endured. She was as sure of that as she was sure the sun would rise tomorrow. Which suited her just fine, since she had the same plan for him.

She didn't manage to leave before the end of the funeral. She would have caused a distraction if she tried to slip away. Once everything ended and the first few rows made their way down the middle aisle, she did her best to weave through the sea of the bodies to get out quickly. She had just about made it to the doors when a hand grabbed hers and pulled her against the wall out of the way of people trying to make their way to the exit. Tad's eyes met hers.

"Thanks for coming. I tried to look around too in between everything, but thankfully all of the officers from our precinct were advised by the captain before the viewing yesterday to refresh themselves on the age progressed photo so there could be eyes everywhere in case this guy showed up."

She didn't correct him that William wouldn't be there.

"Are you coming to the house afterwards for food and stories? You might hear something useful that I didn't think to tell you."

She declined his offer and advised him that she had everything she needed.

"Before I forget, because we kinda got to get moving: what time are you going into the office on Monday? I was thinking about being there at eight since that's the normal work hours, but I didn't know if you liked to get an earlier or later start."

She met his gaze and opened her mouth to speak, but he cut her off.

"Sorry, I wanted to spare you the whole 'I work alone' speech I'm sure you were just about to send my way. I'm sure since we're at the funeral you would have tried to be gentle, but let's skip ahead. I already met with both of our captains after you left on Friday and I'm officially your partner effective immediately. I thought your captain would have already told you, but I can tell by your face that he hadn't broken that news to you quite yet. So, I'm meeting you on Monday. Tell me what time. Also, since I was decent enough to bring you good coffee when you came to my department, I would appreciate the same gesture. I'm sure your department's coffee is just as bad as ours." He tried to smile but it fell short of the 100 watts that normally crossed his face. His gaze slid to the doors where a person stood looking at him, trying to hurry him along.

"Eight is fine." She mentally reminded herself to call the captain once she got into her car and tear her godfather a new one for not giving her the heads up. This is the second time he's failed to divulge necessarily information, and it made her look like an idiot.

"Great. I'll see you then. I got to go, but text me if something changes."

She nodded her head and watched him walk out of the doors. That man had no idea what he was stepping into. She wondered how far she could manage the investigation with him without telling him everything because once he knew, she was sure that he wouldn't look at her the same way. Fear and disgust would fill his face. She wasn't sure why, but she couldn't stand the idea of those blue eyes looking at her that way.

She walked to her car a couple of blocks away and got inside. Thank God for remote start in this blistering Georgia heat. She pushed the button on her steering wheel and told the automated voice to call her captain as she backed out of her parking space and hit the road toward home. It rang a couple of times before going to voicemail.

"Captain, call me back and soon. I have a quite the drive ahead of me, and the longer you make me wait and stew on the fact that you were just going to ambush me on Monday with my new partner, the angrier I'm going to get... and you don't want to make me wait until tomorrow's family lunch at your house after church. Anyway, tell Monica hi and I love her. Let me know what I need to bring. Love you."

As she drove home, her mind shifted to the memory of when she'd learned the truth and how her world turned upside down.

After the murder of the first 3 families...

"Kristen, you have to tell her!"

"Why should I have to tell her, Robert?" Angela's mother sat back in her high back chair and gave him the most nonchalant stare she could muster.

He pointed a finger at her. "You damn well know why and don't give me that look."

"We don't know anything for certain, and what is the point of pulling out skeletons from the closet if we don't have to. She has no idea that Jackson isn't her father, let alone that she has a half-brother somewhere out in the world doing God Knows What."

Robert pinched the bridge of his nose and sighed. He didn't want to show her, but came prepared because he somehow knew that he would have to do it. He opened the manilla envelope he'd put on the coffee table earlier and pulled the picture from inside, sliding it across the table to face her. She glanced at it before reaching out and turning the picture over in disgust. She couldn't deny the killer's note to Angela.

It's all fun and games until parents come in and separate the children for playing too well together. Don't you think we're playing together just fine? I do.

—A

"Every note keeps getting more and more obvious. He wants her to know who he is and I want her told before we put out a press release acknowledging that we have a lead suspect and give out William's information. And before you shut all this down because it'll ruin everyone's reputation, we are not releasing their connection to the public. The fact that we know his name should indicate to him privately that she is aware of who he is to her without causing complications for her or her career. All anyone has to know is that he's obsessed with her. Thankfully, William's mother never put a father on the birth certificate so they shouldn't be able to put it together that they share the same father. Besides, your family took great pains to completely erase any shred of evidence anyone except Jackson was her father. No one was allowed to even whisper about your first husband without your parents having them shunned from the social scene back in the day. But besides all that, and let me be perfectly clear here: if you don't tell her, then I will. And the fall out will absolutely be worse than it would be coming from her mother's mouth."

She glared at him.

"You can be mad at me. And believe me, it breaks my heart to have to tell her that her hero isn't her father. But our hand is being forced here."

"Fine. When do we tell her?"

"Tomorrow after work so she has the entire weekend to process this. I think Stephen should be here for this as well since she's going to tell him anyway, and she's going to need him to be there for her."

"No, I think we need to tell her alone. We also need to tell her that she needs to keep that piece of information to herself. Like you said, if it gets out then it will tarnish her, and Stephen's already halfway out the door as it is according to her. No sense in getting him involved."

Robert clenched and unclenched his fist a couple of times in order to keep his opinion of the man from spewing between his lips. He managed to utter, "I can't say I'm surprised."

"So, tomorrow night the three of us will sit down and have the conversation that I never wanted to have with my daughter. I'll make sure that Maggie goes to the store for something stronger than wine tomorrow morning. I do believe we're all going to need it."

Once she walked Robert out the door, Angela's mother began to prepare herself for the conversation. She went over what she was going to say in her mind at least a hundred times within each hour. She couldn't manage to sleep. She spent most of the night in her sunroom staring out into the dark. Once it was finally time for her to begin getting ready for the day, she changed her outfit at least a dozen times. As if it mattered what she wore. But it did; she knew that whichever outfit she chose, she would never wear again, because she and Angela would always remember it as the outfit she wore when she turned her daughter's world upside down. She and Angela were never close by any means, but this might just tear them apart. In that moment she envied her dead husband, as he wouldn't have to face any of what was coming. Though, Angela and her husband were always thick as thieves. He probably wouldn't get the same level of her wrath anyway. She twirled her wedding rings as she sat in the armchair of her library. She never resented their relationship. After all, she was the one who picked the wrong man to be Angela's father the first time. She didn't dare complain about their relationship when her husband was the father that he didn't have to be towards her. He never felt he needed another one despite Kristen's longing to give him a biological child. She and Angela were all he'd ever need he said. Who was she to feel left out when it came to the two of them?

The clock struck five and she ran her hands down her skirt trying to flatten out the imaginary wrinkles in her outfit. She knew it was time to face her daughter. Angela would be following Robert here in her car. He told Angela that they all had something to discuss but wouldn't divulge further information. According to Robert, Angela believed they were discussing some sort of security plan since she knew her mother and Robert were afraid of this killer's obsession with her. Robert didn't correct her because he wanted her to focus through her work day. She heard her daughter call out "Knock-knock" as they entered the house. Kristen decided to have the conversation in the sunroom despite the library or the living room having the best seating. She called out for them to meet her there. Maggie already laid out three empty glasses and the whiskey in a glass decanter before she left. Kristen wanted privacy, so she advised the staff that they would have the night off. Maggie, the dedicated housekeeper that she is, didn't pry. She just lightly squeezed Kristen's wrist and told her she could call her if she needed anything.

"Oh this doesn't look foreboding at all, Mother," said Angela, as she walked into the room. Kristen was already picking up a glass and pouring herself a drink. Might as well start now. Robert sat down in the chair next to Kristen, and Angela made herself comfortable across from them on the couch. She turned her head to look at the scenery outside. Two hummingbirds fought for dominance at the feeder. Angela set up three or four of those things over the years so she wouldn't have to watch them go at each other. But, they always did at that one feeder by the window. Angela always pondered why, but Kristen knew that some animals were genetically predispositioned to fight and try to obtain dominance. She saw it everyday in the WASP world. Robert cleared his throat to begin but Angela spoke before he could open his mouth.

"You both know that I am a homicide detective. I can protect myself. I don't need any type of extra security because of this sicko. No other officer would ever receive extra security if they were in my place. Stephen has already begun to take measures for his own safety. He's scared, but we have it covered. We beefed up security at the house. I have been teaching him to shoot. Regrettably, for a man born and raised in the South like he is, he isn't a very good shot." She chuckled.

"Your security isn't the discussion," Robert chimed in.

"Then what is the discussion?"

Robert looked at Kristen, who finished off her drink before speaking. She poured herself another before pouring one for Angela and handing it to her. Angela didn't object, but she didn't take a sip either. She just held it on the arm rest while she waited for the news that was causing her mother so much upset.

"Robert advised me that information about this case will be going public soon due to facts being uncovered." She watched her daughter's confused gaze shift to her captain's face over what information about her case could possibly warrant a family meeting. "But, before it went public, you needed to be told certain things. Not all of what we discuss will leave this room. In fact, the only information leaving this room will be the name of the man who is hunting these families and who is writing notes to you." She put up her hand to silence her daughter. "I understand you're confused, but everything will be answered in time. You can't interrupt me because I don't know if I have the strength to continue if I stop talking." Angela shut her mouth and waited. Kristen took a deep breath and retold the story she had been telling herself over and over all day.

"I need to start off by telling you that Jackson—your father—is not your biological father. I met your biological father, William, when I was in college. He came from the wrong side of the tracks, but he was smart and quiet, and he didn't party like the rest of the boys in school. He majored in accounting, so he had my father's approval from the beginning. My father—your grandfather—wanted someone stable for me and who is more stable than a man who's going to be an accountant? We dated for seven months before I became pregnant with you. We were married quickly. My parents set it up that we all went on a ski vacation and came back married. We all said that we couldn't help but take advantage of the trip, that the view was just too beautiful to waste, and that we wanted to start a family right away. Of course there were suspicions about the real reason, but no one brought those forward. Not to my family's face at least. It helped that your grandfather was a powerful man in the social scene. Your grandmother was a force to be reckoned with with the wives as well.

Not long after you were born, William's behavior began to change. He went from having a nightcap or two before bed to getting drunk. He kept staring at you in your crib, and not in a way that a doting father gazes at his child. He stayed longer and longer at work and became more and more withdrawn. I just thought that he struggled being a new parent at first. Then I became convinced he was having an affair. So, I left you with your nanny one afternoon, determined to find out just what exactly was going on with him. I went to his work office first. I assumed that if any evidence was going to be anywhere, it would be there. There was evidence, just not what I thought. I found medication from a doctor I didn't recognize. I had no idea what they were. I took the medication and then searched his home office where I found a journal hidden away. Your father had written awful things inside. Just awful.

When he came home that night, I confronted him. He admitted to everything. He told me that he was having delusions and was being treated by a doctor out of town and paying with cash. He was drinking on top of the drugs to help him cope, but he thought that he was mostly ok. I asked him about the journal. He told me that he had been journaling on and off for years. This wasn't the first time that he had seen a professional about these delusions, and he found journaling to be a good outlet. He did not believe that he was a danger to us because of the medication. I remember throwing the journal at him and calling him a liar because the journal said differently. I threw him out that night. I told him that I no longer wished to see him and that I would be filing for a divorce the very next day. I told him that he had no right to you and that if he fought me on it, I would take him to court and make sure that everything regarding his mental state came out.

He of course then did not fight me during the divorce proceedings. He did however, try to contact me a couple of times afterwards to see you, but I never called him back— and he never pushed it further. I was still scared of him so I went to the local police station to get advice about a restraining order. That's where I met your father Jackson. You were less than a year old at that point. Obviously, when Jackson pursued me, I was more weary than I was with William. But your father convinced both myself and your grandparents pretty quickly that he was my knight in shining armor, as he remains to this day God rest his soul. He and Robert tracked down William after your father and I were married, and ensured that he signed over rights.

It was Jackson's Christmas gift to me that first year we were married. I'll never forget it. Jackson adopted you immediately afterwards, and the rest is history."

Tears ran down Angela's cheeks, but she didn't open up her mouth to speak. She just sat in the chair with her back straight up, expressionless. Kristen expected her to explode, but she should have known better. At her core, Angela's high-breeding always won out and she grew silent instead of acting out.

Robert took over afterwards. "It was imperative that your mother tell you this story so you had the background for this information. Information that your mother didn't have until she went looking for the evidence in William's drawers and in his journal. William had another child. He also admitted that he didn't have anything to do with that child or the mother. She was the ex-girlfriend before your mother."

"I only knew her name previously and that he described her as crazy and toxic for him," her mother chimed in.

"The child's name is William Richards. We don't have much information about him. Once he left high school, he pretty much stayed off the grid somehow."

"So you think he's the killer doing all of this, and why he's obsessed with me," the words croaked out of Angela's lips.

Robert nodded in response.

Her mind began to process their words. "The notes... The notes make so much sense now." She leaned forward and put her face in her hands. "Oh God. It makes so much sense.

He's been hinting at being my brother from the very first note." She gasped. "And the families! The younger sisters—oh God!" She shook her head and then leaned forward as if to get up but Robert stopped her.

"Detective—" he wanted to ensure that she was aware that he was speaking as her captain now, not her godfather. "Detective, much like our godfather/goddaughter relationship isn't spoken about in the office, this information regarding William should not be discussed, not even with Stephen."

Angela wasn't having any of it. "What do you mean even with Stephen? He's my *fiancé* for God's sake! How do you expect me to not tell him? You two just dropped an atomic bomb on everything I know! You just told me that the man who raised me and was everything that I looked up to wasn't my father. And that the man who created the other half of my genetic makeup was crazy. Oh, but let's not forget that my half-brother is also crazy and is murdering families TO GET MY ATTENTION!"

Angela broke down in sobs. Her mother tried to comfort her, but Angela sprung from the couch with her hands out in front of her to ward off any touching, and then walked out of the door. Robert stopped her mother from going after her. He told her to give her daughter time, and that Angela was right. They had done enough for tonight.

That night when Angela arrived home, Stephen's stuff was gone. She found a note left on the bed. He was taking that job his company offered him on the other side of the country. His plane would leave in the morning and he would be staying with his parents tonight so they didn't have to do this face to face. He loved her but he couldn't keep living like this with someone after her and him terrified for his own safety and his family's safety. She fell into bed and looked up at the ceiling, numb. She couldn't manage tears for Stephen because she had been seeing this coming for the last few weeks. At least now she didn't have to try to hide all the family secrets from him. She just assumed he would have the balls to actually end things in person.

"I guess I gave him too much credit," she said aloud to Gizmo as he jumped on the bed to comfort her. She didn't think she would get any sleep that night, but after a couple of minutes, she drifted off into a dreamless slumber.

10

Alexander left his car a couple of blocks from the house and took up his jog down the neighborhood sidewalk. This is his third jog through the neighborhood since that day at the park. He planned to start coming here at least a couple of days a week so no one will look twice at him. He would just be another background piece in the architecture of the community. He never waved, but instead nodded to others when they noticed him, like proper Southern upbringing dictated. The family's house sat at the corner of the cul-de-sac. White house with gray shutters. Wrap around porch and a well-manicured lawn. No white fence according to the 360-view on his Internet map search, and from what he could see on his runs, but it's close enough to the American Dream. No dog either, a major stroke of luck. Their previous pet had just recently died, and they "haven't had the heart to rescue another one yet," according to their social media account. Alexander couldn't help rolling his eyes at that post.

"But what perfect timing," he smiled to himself.

He'd gotten into a routine with baby sister. She expected four months of silence so he could hunt. Though, he'd warned her that he had to keep it fresh and frankly he didn't want to keep waiting anymore. He'd already found the family he wanted next. Why wait so long? Why not cut the time in half? It's not like he needed four months. Before this game, he indulged himself whenever he wanted to. Some days he just walked around the supermarket and picked out a pretty girl who caught his eye. Others, he would find himself a street rat and really take his time in the comfort of his own space. No one looked for those types. Or heard them scream.

He made his way to their house in the cul-de-sac and jogged past it. Once he reached the other side, he faked "hitting the wall." He crouched over, breathing deeply. In through the nose and out through the mouth. He stretched his body and rolled his neck in a circle while he looked at the house. No cars in the driveway, but they had a two-car garage, so they could feasibly be home. He doubted it though. No lights on in the house. No signs of life. The kids were of course in some sort of expensive day camp. Alexander couldn't remember the name of the camp, but he remembered seeing the parents posting about it on social media. Bragging seemed to be the only use the Jones' had for social media. The parents constantly wrote about how the kids had perfect attendance, perfect grades, and extracurriculars out the ass, designed to get them into some expensive Ivy League school. The last name of Jones really fit for this family. He stretched his hamstrings and continued to take in the house. No security sign in the yard. Why bother when they live in such a safe, upper-class neighborhood? He finished his stretches and continued jogging. Another couple of weeks or so of jogging to get to know the routine and then he would enter the house to get the layout. He didn't like surprises. Even when he hunted at his whim, he planned before indulging. He'd been burned before by a surprise, and it turned out messier than it should have. That was years ago when he was still learning, though. Playing with more than one takes longer, more detailed planning—that's all.

He reached the car and got inside. Printed flyers sat in the passenger seat floorboard. If he wasn't able to get up to the house without being noticed another way, he would use a previous ploy of posting up some sort of flyer on the telephone poles. He didn't want it to come to that though. Ploys like that tend to make you more seen rather than just jogging through the neighborhood.

On his way back to the hotel, he stopped by Angela's house. It sat empty. He figured she was still working at the previous police station like she did after he played with a family. How easy would it be to just break in and wait for her? He imagined licking her blood off his knife as he talked to her and told her all the stories that he wanted to share with her. He wanted to hear her thank him for making her career by gifting her with these families. Soon it wouldn't just be her career that he elevated. He and baby sister will be immortalized forever. He stared at her bedroom window and thought about all the future events that would lead up to the end of their game. He grew tired of hiding and waiting for her to find him. She wasn't playing fast enough for his liking. But, what could he expect? Big brothers often grew weary of playing with their little sisters. His eyes darted around, making sure nobody saw his car sitting so close to Angela's for too long, then shifted the car back into drive and drove away.

He reached the extended-stay hotel and went by the front office. He needed to go ahead and pay for next month before anyone came knocking on his door. He pulled out the crisp dollar bills out of his wallet and counted out $800. He made sure that he always paid in sequential, crisp bills so staff thought that he went to the ATM to pull the rent money. He didn't want them suspecting anything different, or they would poke around his room. They might find the rest of the money he had stashed in there. He might have no feelings of love toward his grandmother, but renting out her house under another name instead of outright selling it like he'd originally intended to do four years ago came in handy. According to legal documentation, he sold the house to a "Michael White," and now he is listed as the owner and landlord so the property couldn't be traced back to Alexander. The old lady that rented out the place didn't know how to use the Internet, so she paid to a PO Box he visited once a month. If somehow Angela managed to track down that information and go looking at the post office's security tapes, she wouldn't find anything. She only had a general idea of what he looked like, and he always faced away from the cameras. He also went during the busiest hours of the day for the post office, so there was too much traffic for her to pinpoint him even if he fucked up and the camera actually caught something besides the back of his head or the top of his hat.

He walked up to the girl sitting at the front desk. This one he hadn't run across yet during his stay. He wondered if she was new or if she was a college kid they regularly hired back to assist during summer breaks since she looked college-age. The TV in the small lobby was on, and she directed her gaze to the news reporter while the subtitles rolled across the bottom of the screen. He glanced at the TV to see what held her attention and saw that they were replaying the story about the Reed family. He suppressed a smile and placed a frown on his face instead. He wondered if the captain planned to hold another press conference soon and if Angela would join him. He hadn't done one in a while, not since upper brass tried to take Angela off the case and ruin his fun.

"He is one sick son of a bitch," the girl commented. She caught herself. "I apologize. That was unprofessional of me."

He shook his head. "No no. You're quite alright. You're right though. He is one sick son of a bitch. I hope he's caught soon."

"Me too. Do you think they'll catch him alive?"

"Oh I think a man like that isn't going to let himself get taken alive."

"Maybe you're right. What can I do for you today, sir?"

He gave her his best smile and she blushed. "Oh I just came to pay for next month." He told her his room number and handed her the bills.

"Here for business or pleasure, sir?" She asked him while she looked up his information.

"A bit of both actually. I got a bit of a family reunion coming up soon but me and the family don't get along so well so instead of staying with them, I'm enjoying the pleasure of your company." She looked up from the screen and he winked at her.

The blush deepened. She printed out his receipt and held it out to him.

"Ma'am, unless it's got your phone number on it, I don't need a receipt." Before she could react, he gave her another one of his best smiles and walked out. If he wasn't on a mission, he would have set up a date with her. He bet she was a good lay. He pictured his hands wrapping around her throat and her moaning in pleasure. After, he would watch the fear take over her eyes as he slit her from ear to ear. He sighed. The indulges he gave up for his sister.

He walked back to his room and pulled out his journal, then began to write down what he saw today while researching the Jones family. He wrote about how no one in the neighborhood seemed to be home and his plan to get into the house. He then wrote about going by his sister's house. Things the public will want to read later. He even wrote about the girl in the lobby. Will she read his words later and will a shiver run down her spine at how close she came to death? How she flirted with him not knowing that the smile across his face came from imagining her dead underneath him? His father backed down from being remarkable, but he wouldn't. He leaned back in his chair and thought about the plan he had for the Joneses.

11

ngela walked into the precinct with coffee and crullers. She walked down the hallway to her usual conference room, but she paused when she saw that the light was already on inside. Her brows furrowed at the the sight of someone sitting in a chair just staring at her murder board. She opened the door, ready to tell off whoever was in the room, but the person turned around and flashed their 100 Watt smile.

"I got here early. Your captain let me in. Oh! Are those doughnuts?"

She slid the box to him.

"Do you have a preference? I know I normally calls dibs on one in my head when I bring in baked goods."

She shook her head as she dug into the bag for cream. She found her two creams and then pushed the bag his way. She noticed him watching.

"What?"

"Nothing. When I brought coffee, you took it black. But this time you're adding cream."

"Well, normally I take it black but their coffee is a darker roast than most, so I need a little cream to cut some of the bitter taste. I don't use sugar because these doughnuts have more than enough sugar for my daily intake."

He took a bite and his eyes closed as he moaned. "But damn are they delicious."

"Yes, delicious..." she trailed off. Her gaze stuck on his face as he savored the taste. She shook her head to clear refocus herself. "How was the rest of the weekend?"

He shrugged. "As you would expect." He turned his attention to the board clearly avoiding any further discussion on the matter. "So, Captain Armstrong sent me your official file after he approved me as your partner and I examined this board. I think I'm caught up on everything. What's the plan for today?"

"I normally start off by adding the most recent victims to the board."

He pointed to the right top corner of the board. She saw his partner's information and pictures taped up. Of course he add the family photo to the top.

"Ok, I then normally type up any lingering documentation, which ironically is completely finished. After that, I pour over the families and see if there are any similarities to them."

"So far what do the families have in common?"

"Other than the fact that they're a two parent household with an older son and younger daughter, they don't seem to have anything in common. Their paths don't seem to cross at all. But, that doesn't mean we won't find anything. I wonder if we received a copy of the 911 call yet. I remember you saying on the first day that you would get with Becky but I haven't seen it before now and she promised it no later than today. I didn't check over the weekend though." She took out her laptop and began to boot it up.

"Remind me again about the 911 call."

"Yes, so, the call is another key piece of evidence that this is the same killer. He always calls around the time of the murder. It varies in regards to him calling before or after he makes the kill, but he always calls. We may not have an updated photo of him, but we have his voice on tape and I would know it anywhere at this point."

"The captain didn't include those in the files he gave me."

"I'm sure he didn't. You don't need to hear those since you have the notes."

"Is this going to be a continuous thing?" He sighed.

"Is what going to be a continuous thing?"

"You tiptoeing around me and not treating me like an equal partner."

She sighed as she looked up from her computer screen and gestured to the murder board. "This was your partner. Your best friend. Your family. You shouldn't even be on this case. I don't know why our captains are even allowing you to work on this case, especially my captain."

"Says the detective that at one point was going to be taken off the case because there was suspicion that you in fact had a personal connection to this killer and it's why he's focused on you in whatever this is." He said pointedly.

"That is completely different." She lied.

"Maybe. But no one wants to find this guy as much as you do except for me. I am also bringing fresh eyes to this case. You've been staring at these faces for two years. I haven't."

"There is a reason no one wants to work with me on this case."

"I don't have a family that I'm worried about protecting. He already took mine."

Those words hit harder than any blow to the face.

"It's offensive that you think I can't compartmentalize my grief enough to catch this sick fuck."

She turned her attention to the board again. Kelly's smiling face stared back at her. "You're right. I am just used to doing everything alone since I've been doing it from the beginning. The last time he thought someone was trying to encroach on this investigation, he carved a message in a little girl's stomach." Her eyes trailed over to the Finch family photo before she refocused her attention back to Tad. "But, you're right and I'm sorry. I promise moving forward I will do my best to treat you more like a partner. You have to promise me though that if you need a time out at any point during this investigation you tell me."

He nodded in agreement, and they shook hands on it.

She woke her computer from its screensaver mode and checked her email to see if the 911 dispatch call came in. She forwarded a copy to Tad and then opened up the audio clip. These older government issue laptops took a minute to pull up an audio file. They waited for it to load and then the recording began. The operator's voice started the recording with the standardized 911 greeting. Angela heard William's voice answer. The familiar, calm cadence. He gave the address of the family and stated that there had been a murder. The operator asked him how he knew and attempted to keep him on the phone. William just stated plainly that he knows because he killed them. He repeated the family's address once more before the call line went dead. The operator used the caller ID to attempt a callback and of course it rang to the burner phone William left on the side of the road just a few houses down. Angela got the phone transferred into evidence at her station since she took over handling the case. The phone was dusted for prints but it showed up clean. Just like the identical phones she already had in the evidence box.

"Does every call sound like this?" Tad asked.

"His voice is the same in every call but sometimes he calls before the murder as I said earlier. Sometimes he calls after the murder like this one."

Tad put on gloves and took the phone out of the evidence bag. He turned it on and looked up call history. "Does each phone only have the 911 call in the call history?"

"Yep. We tried to have crime techs look to see if maybe he had made previous calls but then erased them before he tossed it. No luck. Crime techs couldn't pull any more information from the phones."

"No way to trace the phones to a store and check the tapes?"

"These are the popular minute phones they sell in every gas station and quick shop you can walk into. It doesn't help that he has murdered the families in different counties so he could have purchased bulk or a couple at time, etc."

Angela watched Tad examine the evidence box. A small wrinkle appeared between his eyebrows as he concentrated. His eyes slowly moved back and forth along the contents of the box to ensure he mentally cataloged everything. Stubble had begun to peek out along his jawline. She guessed that he didn't take the time to shave before he made the trek out to her precinct. She wondered what it would feel like to brush her knuckles across the stubble. *What is wrong with you?* She mentally scolded herself for her childish, schoolgirl thoughts and reminded herself that this man just lost his family. The last thing either of them needed to be thinking about was something other than the case in front of them. His eyes darted up to hers. The whisper of a smile crossed his face like he knew what she was thinking. She scowled and turned her attention back to her laptop. Despite there being a recording, she would need to add the contents of the call to her notes. She pulled up a blank document and began to type up the report.

"So, after you type up the report, what are we going to do?"

"I know you said that you went over all of the evidence and you have been examining the board, but I thought we would go over everything again. I could walk you through it all seeing as you're the fresh eyes on the case and all." She didn't need to look up to know that he had a surprised look on his face.

"Oh so you've got jokes now, huh?" Tad chuckled.

She just put a finger to her lips before continuing to type.

Tad took advantage of the time to take out everything from the box and put it neatly in front of them on the table. He'd told her that she would warm up to him and based on the joke he was right. She was beginning to thaw, if only slightly. It was just the two of them until the end or until the captain sent him back. Captain Armstrong agreed to a probationary transfer pending his usefulness to Angela. She didn't need to know that though. Her captain gave him the file when they met on Friday once he pled his case. He poured over the contents all weekend and searched through all the news reported online except for when he attended the viewing and funeral. Like everyone, he and Nick had been keeping up with the case, but it didn't hurt to go over the details reported along with the official report. He couldn't put a finger on how he knew that this was just the "official" information, but he knew there was more. There had to be more. Assumptions made and details given that went beyond the scope of good detective work. He wondered if that was why top brass came in at one point and tried to take this case from her. Not that it worked. He studied her features out of the corner of his eye. He thought her prettier in person than in the press conferences and the pictures in the newspaper articles. Her eyes bluer and with just a hint of another color around the pupils. A light dusting of freckles adorned her nose and checks. Her lips fuller than the pictures. He never told Nick how captivating he found her. He joked with Nick about it, but he never told him the truth. Despite all the cop talk and the articles suggesting her ice queen disposition, he continued to see the unwavering heartbreak in her eyes. The captain's too, but only when he looked at Angela when she wasn't looking. He was determined to find out everything. Nick and June and his godchildren deserved everything.

He returned his focus to the evidence in front of him once he laid it all out before them. There wasn't much. He examined the suspected face of the killer. He wondered how close the age progressed photo resembled what this psycho actually looked like in person. He imagined he altered his appearance at least with a dye job once his face went all over the news stations. Tad continued to etch the picture into his brain when Angela said "done."

"There isn't much here. Not for six crime scenes and twenty-four bodies."

"Unfortunately, he doesn't give us much to go on. He leaves no prints. He has no connection with any family as far as we can determine." She tapped on one of the notes in its evidence bag. "He leaves me notes as you can see, but not any details in those notes that can lead us to him."

"I thought you guys had that fingerprint...the one that made you all decide it was this man." He tapped on William's photo.

"Well, yes." The lie rolled off her tongue with all the practice she had when the brass came to town. Robert made her repeat the cover story over and over until she could pass a lie detector test regarding her knowledge. "We obtained a latent print during the third crime scene. We weren't even sure if we had enough of a print to get anything when Cap and I ran it through the database. What popped up was William's juvenile file. Unfortunately, somehow during packaging, moisture contaminated the print, so we no longer have the actual evidence, just the results." He must be more suspicious than most, or more observant, because a flash of disbelief crossed his face before he masked it and shook his head indicating understanding.

"And this guy is a ghost in the modern age, huh?"

"Looks like it. The last picture of his was from senior year of high school. He has no property in his name. His grandmother's house was sold sometime after she passed away. No bank accounts in his name. No other relatives. I would be willing to bet that he has his stuff in another name, but that's just a guess."

"So pretty much when you come back to your office, the case goes cold until another family dies."

Her eyes narrowed and her lips became a thin line. He held up his hands in front of him in mock surrender. "That wasn't a knock at you or your detective skills. I was just saying that that's pretty much is what happens."

"I still work it. This is the only case on my load. We still get tips from the tip line, so I investigate those. But, yes at this point, the investigation hasn't had much progress in locating William."

"If his name is William, why does he sign the notes 'A?'" Tad asked.

"I can only speculate. Cap and I believe it's a reference to his middle name, Alexander, but obviously we cannot confirm this since we've never had a conversation with William." She stood up and stood beside him at the table. "Shall we start at the beginning then?"

He gestured toward the evidence. "Be my guest."

12

He met Ashli "with an I" at a college campus party. He didn't attend college, but that didn't stop him from pretending he did on Friday nights while he prowled around different campuses. This particular one happened to be in Tennessee while driving back to Georgia. Despite her sorority looks and sorority name, she majored in history where she intended on one day being a professor in the subject. He introduced himself by his middle name and she answered with, "Alexander. Like Alexander the Great." She saw the puzzled look in his expression and spent the rest of the night regaling him with details regarding this king. Alexander sat in the chair, immersed in her words and he thought to himself how she had picked the right path for herself. She would've made a great professor. Too bad she met him instead.

A couple more hours and a few more drinks later, he walked her to her car. She fiddled with keys trying to prolong the moment, expecting a kiss. He pulled her close and pressed his lips to hers. She tasted of the hunch punch she drank at the party with a hint of young girl innocence. He deepened the kiss as he slid the knife pulled from his pocket into her stomach. He inhaled her surprise and swallowed her muffled scream. He pushed her up against the car and twisted the knife slowly before dragging it up toward the rib cage. She attempted to push him away, but her weakening body couldn't compete against him. He kissed down her throat and felt her heartbeat against his lips. He savored the last beats before she sagged, lifeless against him. He pulled the knife from her body and returned it to his pocket. He kept his chest pressed to hers to keep her up as he pulled surgical gloves from the inner pocket of his jacket. He snapped them on before he opened the car door and placed her body in the backseat so that if anyone came by, they would think that she passed out drunk. He laid a jacket he found in the floorboard over her and curled up her legs so it looked more real. He shut the door and removed his gloves. He put them back in his pocket to be disposed of later. He zipped his jacket to hide her blood on his shirt and walked to his car that wasn't more than a few aisles away. He thought about her comparison between him and Alexander the Great. He only went by Alexander while hunting, but he thought maybe he should adopt it full time. After all, he never liked William. Never felt like a William, especially since his grandmother called him William instead of Will when he was in trouble. She would almost spit the name from her mouth and remind him that he was a good-for-nothing just like his namesake. Two years later, when he found out just how much alike he and his father actually were, he vowed that he would never go by William again. He was better than the father who never had the balls to be great.

———

Alexander's mind snapped back to the present as he parked his car in front of the empty house two streets down from the Jones' home. He didn't know why that moment in time came to his mind, but he guessed some good memories just float to the surface sometimes, like dead bodies that have been sunk in water. He had the Jones' routine down now that he'd been jogging the area for the last two months. He knew the neighbors would not be home either. Everyone went to work and came home about the same time each day like something out of a movie. Despite the father being a lawyer, he didn't work late at the office often. He preferred to work from the home office late in the evening. The children had extracurricular activities, but the whole family sat together every evening at the table for dinner. He planted a tiny camera on the corner of one of the large dining room windows after about a week of jogging around the neighborhood. He also planted one near the front door so he could get a timeline of when they would be home. Later, before he left the scene and called 911 to alert the police of this family's demise, he would pocket them and wipe the windows so no evidence of his camera's existence could be found. Tricks of the trade learned over time. The new stalking brought to you by technology. Some things you can't learn from technology alone unfortunately. Sometimes, you just got to get your hands dirty.

He jogged to the next street over from the Jones' house and cut through the yard of the house behind them. He put on the disposal gloves from his pocket before he picked the lock on the back door and opened it. *Beep. Beep.* The alarm on the door went off. A great deterrent for someone trying to break in and doesn't know any better. It gives the illusion of an actual alarm, but it's just more for the parents to know if the kids are attempting to sneak out the back door at night after everyone went to bed. He bet he could find those same alarms on the windows of the kids' rooms as well. Noah and Sophie were just approaching the age where sneaking out was a thought in their head. He would have to disable those while he was here. It's simple enough really, and he knew how to do it so that the family wouldn't know it had been tampered with unless they tested it. The back door led him into the kitchen. To the left was the pantry that led into the garage. He reminded himself to lock that door when he snuck in next time just in case. Past the kitchen led him into the formal dining room—because of course they had a large, formal dining room that surely hosted a lot of dinner parties along with their nightly family dinners. He'd seen the room from outside, but seeing it up close revealed just how grand and imposing this room truly was within the home. This room led into the living room where the front entrance was located. Another door he needed to make sure was locked up tight. To the left of the front door were the stairs leading to the bedrooms. The father's office where he worked at night was on the other side of the stairs. The father faced the desk toward the living room so Alexander would have to wait until he saw the office light go off before sneaking in. Alexander faced the stairs. Fourteen stairs. He walked across each step. A couple of the steps squeaked when stepped on in certain places. He thought to himself that this is why he always does a test run—because parents, especially parents to teenagers according to his grandma, tend to hear creaking steps in the middle of the night. He expected Mr. and Mrs. Jones to be particularly light sleepers. He ascended the stairs. To the right, the parents' master suite. To the left, the children's rooms.

He entered the son's room first since it was at the end of the hall and the farthest from the parents' room. He checked the window security first. A smile crossed his face when he examined the alarm. *Clever boy.* He already disabled his alarm, but did so in such a way that the wires could easily be put back together again to make it look as if the alarm was still active. Alexander opened the window. Remnants of cigarette use sat outside, but remained unseen unless someone looked straight down. So Noah was a secret smoker. No big surprise really with a father like that. Alexander bet that dear ol' Daddy had a stash of his own secret cigarettes somewhere himself. Fathers often had their own secrets after all. Alexander grabbed the pack off the outside corner where Noah stashed it and plucked one out. He didn't often smoke. He believed in his body being a temple, but every so often he treated himself. He examined the red package. Cowboy killers. Noah didn't play around. Alexander thought to himself that these would have killed this kid eventually had he not caught Alexander's eye. After putting the pack back exactly how he'd found them, he placed the cigarette on his left ear and continued his search throughout the home.

He moved to the parents' bedroom. He opened the nightstands. A gun lay in the father's drawer. Alexander checked the chamber and clip and found them both empty. He rolled his eyes. No bullets of course, because "no one wants an accident in the house" with the kids around. He wondered where the father put the bullets. He searched around the room but didn't find any. He guessed that the father put the bullets in a safe somewhere in the home. He checked the chamber one more time just to double check there wasn't a chambered bullet. He wondered why families kept guns in the home if they weren't going to put bullets in them. Any empty gun wouldn't scare an intruder because any intruder would have their own actually loaded gun. He shrugged. He guessed he shouldn't complain, since it meant they wouldn't shoot him during the altercation. According to the nightstands, the mother slept on the right side of the bed. Even if she went for the gun, she would have to reach across the bed, and he would already be on her within that time. He left the parents' room and made his way to the daughter's bedroom, his favorite room in the house.

He opened the door to her bedroom. His eyebrows lifted and his mouth fell open. White walls met his gaze. Gray pillows and a gray bedspread. No pictures or artwork on the walls. The only signs of life were pictures of her and her friends taped to the mirror on the closet door.

"Oh, this one has secrets," he said to himself. "No teenager lives like this unless they're hiding who they really are."

He looked around the room. Sophie would know that her mother would search the nightstand and under the mattress. She would check the dresser drawers, especially the underwear drawer. He thought for a moment and examined the room. He looked toward the bed and cocked his head. Now, why would there be scuff marks on the front right corner of the bed? The mom would check under the bed, but she wouldn't need to pull it away from the wall. No scuff marks on the back right under the headboard. He smiled. It couldn't be that easy. He pulled the bed corner toward the doorway. The floorboard that the post previously rested on had a tiny nick at the seam. He pulled out his knife and positioned it in the nick to pull up the floorboard. He placed the piece on the bed and examined the secret hideaway. He picked up a package of cigarettes. What was it with these kids and smoking? At least they weren't cowboy killers. Not that menthol was much better. He dug his hand deeper into the hole in the floor. He pulled out a pocket knife and examined it. He ran the blade across his shorts. It might not have been big, but it was sharp. He pocketed the knife on impulse. He didn't normally take trophies, but he couldn't resist the desire to end her life with her own secret knife. He dug some more. He seemed to find looking at her secrets a good bit of fun. His hand found something large. He wasn't sure how he would manage to get it out from under the floorboard, but he found the board to the right of the hole gave way easily. A journal. A leather journal not unlike his own back at the hotel.

"Oh, this girl is interesting," he said out loud to himself again.

He flipped open the book and found a strip of photo booth pictures between two pages like a bookmark.

"Well, would you look at that. Little Sophie is in a relationship. I bet Mommy and Daddy don't know that your best friend Megan is also your girlfriend."

The timer on his phone went off with buzz in his pocket. He snoozed the alarm and put Sophie's stuff back, aside from the knife he'd pocketed. He needed to walk out now that he understood the layout. He moved the bed back to its original position. Before he left the house, he made sure to tamper with the back door alarm so it wouldn't alert the family next time he came through. He went back to his car and stretched next to it so it looked like he's just come back from his normal jog around the neighborhood. He got back into the car and drove to the extended stay. He pulled out his journal and began to write his observations. A plan began to form in his mind. He pulled out the stolen pocketknife and twirled it in his fingers. An interesting girl deserves an interesting ending after all.

13

Angela looked at Tad across the conference table. He stared at the stack of evidence in front of him as if it changed from all the times of going through it before. A couple of calls came in from the tip line since the last family's murder, but none of them amounted to anything other than wasting their time. She admitted to herself that she has enjoyed the long talks with Tad in the car. The smile that caught her attention when she first met him didn't compare to his laughter as he regaled her with stories of his friendship with Nick and his family. She once told him that he didn't have to talk about them if he didn't want to, after one story had caused pain to cross his face. He just replied that talking about them kept them alive. He still loved them and wanted to talk about them. It helped him miss them a little less. Though, nothing stopped her in her tracks quite like the heat she caught in his eyes more than once when he looked at her. He always covered it quickly, and he hadn't said anything to her, but it was there. She wondered if he ever caught the same look from her. Not that she would act on it. Too much at stake.

She pushed away her thoughts and reminded herself to enjoy the partnership while it lasted, since Tad would go back to his office soon. Just like it always did, the case grew cold between the families, and they had another two months if William kept to his four month timetable. She was certain his captain wouldn't want Tad to be gone too much longer since they weren't making any more progress than she had made before he became her partner.

"Penny for your thoughts?"

Her face changed from a dazed expression to focusing on him. "Huh? What?"

"You get this crinkle between your eyebrows when you're thinking really hard about something. I assume it's not case related since you're just staring over your black laptop screen."

"How do you know my screen is black?"

He pointed to the projection screen on the wall behind her. She smiled and shook her head.

"My bad," she said.

"Case related or not case related?"

"Oh... uh... It's nothing. Just thinking about how you're going to be going back to your station soon since the case isn't moving forward."

"It's only been a couple of months and I've told you that I'm not going anywhere. You're stuck with a partner. And you need one since your case notes are atrocious."

No one ever dared to tease her the way he did, aside from her godfather and her father before he died. Not even her ex-fiancé joked with her like Tad did. A warmth spread within her whenever he teased her.

"Hey, are there any good bars around here? I could really go for a beer tonight."

"We have one. I wouldn't call it particularly good or nothing, but it's all we got around here."

"All we got is better than nothing. What time is it anyway?" He looked at his watch. "Shit, it's almost seven. Why don't we call it a day? Or, if you prefer, we can continue working over some beers. Sometimes Nick and I would be shooting the shit in a bar after work before he went home to June and we would suddenly have an epiphany. That's how it happens sometimes. You relax and let the back of your brain chew on it for a while, and then it spits out an answer."

She yawned and stretched. "I doubt that's going to happen tonight, but it can't hurt. I don't want another family's death on my hands."

He let the comment go. She would talk about that in her own time.

They headed out of the precinct. Angela told Tad to just follow her to her house, and they would ride together after she got changed. He took a moment to admire her house before getting out of the car. He didn't know what kind of home he expected her to live in, but this wasn't it. This was the kind of home that a family lived in, not a single woman. It had the white picket fence in the front yard. A wrap around porch and rocking chairs greeted each guest at first glance. A black fan hung above the chairs to provide assistance against the scorching Georgia heat when you wanted to sit and enjoy sweet tea or a beer outside with company. To the side of the house was a two-car garage. Nick would have taken one look at this house and said that this was the kind of house that a man could grow old with his wife in. June would have loved this house. He bet it even had a stairwell behind the front door. The kind kids ran down to greet their dad after a long day at work. Angela's knuckles tapped on the glass, breaking his concentration.

"You coming in or what, Detective?"

He grabbed his gym bag from the passenger seat and followed her in the house. Of course he was right. Up against the wall to the left adorned a stairwell leading up to the second story. To the right of the front door he saw the main living room.

"This is a mighty fine house you got here, Angela," said Tad.

She thanked him as she made her way down the hallway beside the stairs to the master bedroom that was tucked in beside the kitchen. She opened a little door between the living room and the kitchen as she went past.

"I assume based on the bag that you have clothes to change into. You can use the little half bath there or you can go upstairs into one of the other bedrooms if you want more space. That bathroom is tiny."

Tad peered into the little room. "Now how in the world can anyone fit into that bathroom?"

Her voice carried from behind the closed door. "Beats me, but Stephen insisted the builders of this home were brilliant for putting in this half bath so guests wouldn't use the master bathroom or have to walk upstairs to use the other one."

"Stephen?"

"Ex-fiancé."

"That's right. You mentioned him before. I'm going upstairs." Tad thought about Angela's ex-fiancé on his way up the stairs. He thought back to the media frenzy when it first came out that this killer was stuck on Angela. She said the news reported her engagement even though Stephen wasn't pertinent to the case because they tried to dig up as much information on Angela as they could back in the day. He wondered how long the ex stayed around before he left her alone to handle this psycho. She didn't say when she talked about him briefly, and he didn't think to ask at the time. Tad went into the spare bedroom, changed clothes, and then came back down the stairs. He found Angela in the kitchen with a beer in her hand.

"You know, typically cops don't pre-game and drive drunk to the bar."

"Ha ha," she said sarcastically. "I set us up with an Uber, and the driver should be here in about ten minutes."

"Oh, in that case, let me get a beer then." Angela motioned to the unopened beer in front of her on the kitchen island. Tad opened the bottle and took a huge swig.

"This is a really nice place you've got here, Angela." Tad commented again as he looked around more. "You and Stephen pick it out together?"

"Actually I picked this house out. Well, Mother and I did. Stephen was always working too late to meet us at the houses while we were looking. He would have preferred a big, new build but I insisted on something more homey and charming. A place with a neighborhood already filled with families and kids."

"Spoken like a true Southern lady," he smiled.

"Well, I grew up in the new build golf club neighborhood with gates and older people."

"I thought your dad was a detective. That doesn't sound like cop money."

"He was a detective that didn't come from money. Mother came from money. I've already told you this." She turned away and put her empty beer in the trash can underneath the sink. "You want another one?

"No, I will save the rest of my drinks for the bar. And you told me that she had money, but you didn't say that she was rich."

"Saying someone has money is the polite way of calling someone rich."

He held up his hands in mock surrender. "Fair enough. I guess I just didn't picture you growing up rich, even though you told me that she had money."

"Despite growing up in that kind of neighborhood, my dad kept things very down to earth in the house. Really, the only reason that we lived in that kind of neighborhood was because my parents lived with my grandparents. My grandparents were always away on business trips and whatever else, and they didn't like having to pay someone to keep watch of the house and staff—"

"You had staff?" He choked out as his sip of beer went down hard.

She ignored his shock. "They told them that the house would go to them upon death anyway and they liked having us close. Mother convinced my dad, God knows how, that it would be better. So that's what happened."

Tad whistled. "Let me guess... you met your ex through your grandparents."

She took a sip of her beer, but responded by tapping on the tip of her nose.

"Of course."

"Don't roll your eyes. They didn't push him on me. I just escorted mother to one of those fancy dinners and Stephen and I hit it off. Though I will be honest and say that the captain and Mother didn't love him. Captain thought he wanted to turn me into a little housewife that had nothing better to do than volunteer with whatever charity was popular with the law firm. Mother thought he was after her family's money and connections. But, to their credit, they didn't push their feelings on me. I told them that Stephen really loved me." Bitter laughter escaped from her lips. "They were right of course on both accounts. After Stephen left me, he married the daughter of one of the partners at the firm within the year, and she is content to volunteer on the charity board within the firm." She seemed to catch herself and her eyes grew wide. "I'm so sorry. You didn't ask for all of that. Maybe I should slow down before I get some bar food in me."

Tad shrugged. "No apologies necessary."

He didn't get a chance to ask her more questions before the driver arrived and they made their way to the bar. The driver dropped them off at a little brick pub on the main road. Tad looked around. Sports memorabilia lined the walls above the booths. A fake retro looking juke box stood in the corner playing music that didn't quite seem loud enough.

"There is a second story just up those stairs over there. They have an outdoor patio I like to sit at."

"Of course you do. What cop doesn't like to do surveillance while off the clock?"

She laughed at his teasing. "I prefer to think of it as mild people watching. My best friend Leslie and I used to come here all the time and people watch on her summers off from college. Just follow me."

He followed her up to the second story and they found a table in the corner of the balcony. They ordered two beers and burgers from the waitress.

"So, back to our discussion at your house. When did you and your ex end things?"

"After the Harris family was murdered."

"The Harris family was the third set of victims, right?"

"Correct. Things ended the night before we announced William as our main suspect. I came home and he had left a note on the bed saying that he was going to stay with his family for the night before his flight out in the morning.

He was taking that job across the country." She caught him before Tad opened his mouth to comment. "I don't blame him. Looking back, we had problems before that we kept ignoring. Like I said, ultimately he wanted a stay-at-home wife who came from a family of influence. We talked about me staying at home on multiple occasions. Fought about it really. Then William came along, and it became clear that he had set his sights on me. Stephen didn't sign up for that."

"You sign up for something like that when you fall in love with a cop."

She sighed. "Maybe wives think about stuff like that when they fall in love with a cop; but not men, especially high-powered alpha men."

"Maybe you're just chasing the wrong alpha males then." His gaze went to her lips and heat rose to her cheeks.

"Maybe. But I have no hard feelings anymore about Stephen. Everyone except Cap has had to back off from my life because of William. Too much risk to themselves or their loved ones."

"But he's never gone after anyone you're directly involved with, right? Just innocent families like Nick and June."

"That doesn't mean he won't. You know that. He didn't start out with families. He is picking families now because of me." The second the words came out of her mouth, she wished she could pluck them out of the air and shove them back into her mouth and swallow them back down.

The waitress came back with their food. Angela immediately shoved a big bite of burger into her mouth. Can't answer questions with your mouth full. Tad chuckled.

"I assume based on that T-Rex-sized bite that you don't want me to follow up with why you believe that these families have anything to do with you."

She swallowed the bite with help from a swig of beer. "You always get right to the point of things no matter how uncomfortable, don't you?"

Tad grabbed the ketchup bottle and doused the empty corner of his plate with ketchup. He leaned back thoughtfully as he plucked a fry from his plate and drug it through the red sauce. "Nick used to get onto me all the time because I didn't have any finesse. I ask pointed questions and it often makes people uncomfortable. I don't skirt around to make people feel comfortable in an interrogation."

"Is this what this is? An interrogation?" She teased.

"No, it's not. It's just a conversation between a man and a woman."

His choice of words didn't go unnoticed by Angela. Once again, she could feel her cheeks turning red. No more drinks after this beer. She wouldn't be able to control herself if she kept going. Those long nights working together and chasing leads pushed them close. Aside from her catching Tad looking her over and Tad catching her more than once doing the same, they'd kept their tightness to one that develops between partners. Besides, the moment he found out why his former partner and his family died, that heat would turn to hate, and she couldn't blame him. She and Captain Armstrong couldn't keep this a secret once they caught William. Tad's voice interrupted her thoughts.

"I may ask pointed questions and don't have any finesse, but I know when not to ask a question and let someone get there on their own. Sometimes silence is the best question."

"Sometimes silence is the best choice," she responded.

"Fair enough."

They continued eating together but spoke of easier topics. She told him more stories of her father and their adventures together before he passed. Tad talked more of Nick and June and the kids. She loved how little crinkles formed next to his shining eyes when he spoke of them. Despite the pain that crept in toward the end of his stories, when the truth creeped in around the edges that all their stories together now ended, a genuine love for them kept the smile on his face. Angela reached across the table and took his hand at one point, though she couldn't pinpoint when. His thumb rubbed gently back and forth across the back of her hand. A text came across her screen.

"Oh jeez! It's almost eleven! We need to get back." She pulled up her app and put in for a car to pick them up. "They should be here in about ten minutes."

Tad picked up the tab and they headed back to her place. Tad asked where the nearest hotel was since it was too late to drive home, especially after this many beers. Angela waved her hand in mock annoyance and told him not to be silly. She had a perfectly good guest room upstairs as he well knew. She told him to grab his clothes and she would wash his uniform with hers so he would have clean clothing for tomorrow. He grabbed his clothes from his bag and handed them to her. She asked him if he needed anything else washed while she already had the washer going, and he told her that he didn't. He followed her to the hallway closet so she could give him an unopened toothbrush and toothpaste. She turned around to hand him his toiletries and found his body inches from hers. His arm caressed across her hips to her back and pulled her in so their bodies molded together. His other hand brushed down her jaw, and his thumb outlined her bottom lip. When she didn't pull away, he brushed his lips across hers, testing her. A small whimper escaped her lips. His hands fisted in her hair as he deepened the kiss. All thought left her mind and her knees went weak. Her arms wrapped around his neck as she met his passion with her own. He kissed her like a drowning man who found air on her lips. Reluctantly, he pulled himself back and they came away breathless. His lips brushed hers again. He needed one more taste. His hand moved from her hair to her hips. He didn't know if he was stilling her or himself.

"Wow," he whispered.

She couldn't muster up words so she just shook her head in agreement. He put his forehead against hers and sighed. He turned his wrist to look at the time and groaned.

"We need to get some sleep, honey." His thumb outlined her bottom lip again. She saw the urge to continue kissing her in his eyes. She took her arms from around his neck.

"I'll see you in the morning then."

He didn't remove his hand from her hip. He lightly kissed her lips.

"See you in the morning."

She braced against the doorframe of the closet to steady herself as she listened to his footsteps go up the stairs to the guest bedroom just above her own. She knew she would dream about that kiss.

———

The next morning Tad awoke to a strange, vibrating weight on his chest. He opened one eye and saw a black cat with large, yellow eyes staring at him. Upon seeing him open his eye, the cat began to knead his claws in anticipation.

"Well, hey there." The cat got up and demanded affection with a soft meow and headbutt. He gladly gave into the request. "You're a friendly little guy, huh?" He picked up the cat and carried him along as he made his way down the stairs to retrieve his clothes.

"I see you met Gizmo." He heard Angela call from the kitchen island. "He's such a little ham."

"That's ok. I don't mind being a sucker. I didn't know you had a cat though. How has that never come up?" He gently put him on the floor and Gizmo ran over to his food bowl.

"Yeah, I found him when he was just a tiny, half-dead kitten. I took him to the vet and they told me not to hope for anything. A couple hours later, they called saying that he was good to come home. Despite the backlash I received, I decided to keep him, and he's been a spoiled little man ever since."

"The ex not a fan?"

"Gizmo pre-dates Stephen actually. But, yes. First Mother then Stephen."

"Clearly you won the war there."

"I did." She walked around to the laundry room and came back with his folded clothes. "If you want a shower, there is necessary shower stuff in the guest bathroom and a clean towel hanging over the shower curtain. Coffee?"

"Yes please." He looked at his watch. 7:15 a.m. "My God, woman. What time do you get up in the morning that you're already dressed and ready to go?"

She chuckled. "I get up every morning at six. Like daddy like daughter there. Though my father always made breakfast in the morning. Since it's normally just me, I tend to grab breakfast with my second morning coffee at the coffee shop. Their biscuits are delicious." She handed him his coffee and he took a sip.

"Oh, that's good. So, that's where we're going once we leave here?"

"About that... I think it's a good idea if you just head to the station so we don't walk in together."

"Is that so? Well, honey, you know my car is in your driveway this morning, right? And if anyone asked, we could just say we were working late, and it got too late for me to drive. It's a half-truth anyway."

"I understand that, but I would rather we still didn't show up together."

"Is that right?" He put his coffee down and walked toward her. She saw the determination in his eyes and she backed up into the counter trying to put some place between them. His body met hers and once again she felt herself tingle in anticipation of his touch. "You wouldn't be ashamed of me now, would you?"

She bit her lip. He fought the urge to bend down and bring her lip into his mouth and nibble on it to hear that little whimper again. "I didn't say that."

"Alright then. Why don't you head to the office, and I'll bring breakfast? It's the least I can do since you let me sleep over last night, even if it was not in the bed I wanted to be in."

She felt bold under his gaze. "Then why did you stop?"

"Because we don't need to do police work on no sleep."

Her eyebrow lifted. "You sure are full of yourself aren't you?"

His hand worked up from her hip to just under her breast. Her body arched up to give him better access. He responded with a smug smile. He leaned in and whispered in her ear, "just you wait, honey."

Her fingertips ran across the top of his pants, and it was his turn to lean into her. He closed his eyes and his breath hitched. She turned so her mouth grazed against his ear. Her teeth gently nipped and he moaned, grinding his body against hers.

"Unless you plan on the both of us calling out of work today, I suggest you stop tempting me, woman," he growled.

She slid her body against his as she moved out from under him.

"I'll see you at the station. Lock the door behind you. Make sure you don't shut any doors around here unless you know Gizmo isn't in there. I don't want him stuck in some room all day while I'm at work. I'll text you the address of the coffee shop. You might want to hurry before the line gets too long." She grabbed her bag at the door and he heard the door close behind her.

"*Oh, she's good*," he thought. She knew exactly what she did to him. He took a couple of deep breaths and got himself ready before leaving her house.

———

Angela walked into the station with a smile on her face for the first time in a long time. She couldn't help herself. Tad gave her hope. Hope that they would find William and hope for a future. The kind of hope she had back when her father was around. She thought she found that hope again when she found Stephen, but she knew the truth now. Tad was real, and Stephen was just a distraction. She put her bag down in the conference room. Tad shouldn't be far behind. The shop didn't normally take long, even with a line. She opened her laptop and brought her focus back to work. Despite whatever was growing between her and Tad, it didn't take away the higher purpose. Those families deserved justice.

Tad deserved justice for having his family ripped away from him.

Your fault. The reminder echoed in her head. *It's your fault these families were murdered, and Tad will never look at you the same once he finds out.* She shook her head. She wouldn't think of that now. She just wanted to bask in the hope a little while longer.

"Burns!" Captain Armstrong's voice commanded from his office. He didn't need to stand at the doorway for his order to ring through the station.

"Sir," she said when she walked into his office.

"Close the door and close the blinds."

She shut the door behind her and shut the blinds. She sat down across from him and examined his face. His mouth noticeably dropped in a frown. The crinkles around his eyes were more prominent. He sat without moving. His gaze rested on the papers in front of him. Bad news.

"I received a call today."

"Tad's captain requesting him back at their station?"

"No. It's too late for that."

"What do you mean it's too late for that?"

His gaze met hers. His back stiffened. "I received a call from William."

14

Alexander jogged in front of Angela's house. He liked to occasionally jog in front of her house and wave as she left for work. She always answered with a tight smile and hands up per Southern code of conduct. He wondered if she felt same the pull he did. The instinctual pull of familial blood flowing through their veins. But, this morning another face was locking the front door.

"Now who in the world could that be?" he wondered to himself.

He passed by the house and stopped at the next door neighbor's mailbox. His hands went to his hips and he bent forward as if he were out of breath or hit with a sudden cramp. He could see the man getting into the car in the driveway. He didn't need a uniform for Alexander to peg him as a cop. Though, the shield around his neck confirmed his suspicions. He watched the man leave the driveway and turn in the direction Angela took every morning. Alexander snarled. She was supposed to work alone. She was supposed to be alone. He turned around and jogged in the direction of his car. Once he reached his car, he got inside and slammed the door behind him. He called the station and asked for the captain.

"Armstrong speaking."

"Why is she not alone?" His breath came from his nose like a bull ready to charge.

The captain met his question with silence. He listened to those 911 calls enough with Angela to recognize the voice on the other end of the phone.

"Did you hear me? Why is she not alone?"

"Sir, you're going to have to tell me who you are and who you're talking about. Why is who alone?"

"Don't play dumb with me, Captain. It insults us both." Robert heard a fist slam against something hard on the other end of the line. "Do I have to carve another message into another body before you all understand? Angela is mine! This is between me and her!"

"Now William, you know that Angela is working the case." His voice went a notch higher than a whisper. The tone he learned in negotiations to use when a madman held a gun to a hostage or to a man threatening to jump to his death.

"Then why did I see some other detective leave her house first thing this morning?"

"Now I don't know anything about that, William."

"Once again, you're playing dumb, Captain. It won't take me long to find out who he is and where he lives. You and I both know that." His tone went from raging bull to a calm that made the captain think of a snake about to strike.

"There is no need for any of that, William."

"Then it's simple, Captain. He must go. Baby sister needs to stay focused on the game. We're so close."

"So close to what, William? To the end?"

"No distractions, Captain. I'll carve that into his body."

"Now William—"

"I wonder if he'll last longer than that poor girl. She screamed you know. I had to put my knee on her neck to cut off her screams. She screamed all the way into shock and then passed out from the pain. I licked her blood off the blade. I couldn't resist congratulating myself on being able to get all the words onto that tiny little torso of hers. I'm sure I'll have more than enough room this time."

A dial tone resounded in the captain's ear. He slammed down the receiver with a curse.

Alexander continued back to his hotel after dumping the latest burner into a nearby trash bin. He knew not to go by the police station and copy down the license plate off the car. The captain had likely ordered extra security for that man and that station as soon as he'd hung up the phone on him. No matter. It wouldn't be hard to figure out if he put his mind to it. But, he planned on giving his baby sister another kind of show. He reached the hotel and went inside to the bed. He pulled out Sophie's knife and cleaned the dirt from under his nails. Only a couple of days away now.

———

Angela's face blanched. "What do you mean you received a call from William?"

"He saw Tad leave your house this morning." He held up a hand before she could speak. "I don't care why he was there. That's not important right now. What is important is the fact that William saw him and he called me in a rage. He threatened to carve the words 'no distractions' into his body like he carved into Brooklynn's." He watched her put her head in her shaking hands. He thought she came close to tears, but she steeled herself before raising her face and meeting his gaze. He saw the poison in her eyes as she spoke.

"I told you. I told you both. I said that this would happen. He is not safe, Captain. Send him back."

"It's too late for that and you know it, Angela. Even if he had nothing to do with this from now on, that's assuming he agreed to it—which I don't think he will—he's on William's radar now."

"It doesn't matter what he agrees to if you and Captain Archer order him off the case."

"It does matter. Where is he now?"

"He went by to grab coffee and biscuits for us as a thank you to me for letting him spend the night, since we worked late last night."

The captain's eyebrow went up, but he didn't comment further. She knew that he knew she was lying, but he wouldn't push the issue. Not right now when they had more pressing matters to attend to.

"William doesn't know Tad's name. Frankly, I believe he's smart enough not to go digging for it right now because he knows that I'm going to put everyone on high alert after that phone call. I do still need to call Captain Archer and give him the heads up to put security on Tad tonight after he leaves here."

"So you are sending him back home?"

"Once he comes in, I'm going to have this same conversation with him and he can decide what he wants to do. If he wants to continue, I will send you both to pick up the burner phone. I have techs working on the location as we speak since he never bothers to turn them off. I doubt we will get anything from the phone since we haven't before, but we should check it anyway. You also need to check around and see if anyone spotted him or if there are security cameras anywhere."

"With all due respect sir, I know what I need to do. I just hope that he didn't leave it at or near my house. I doubt my neighbors will answer the door for me if I knock."

He gave her a sympathetic smile. "Go talk with the techs and then wait in the conference room."

"Yes, sir," she nodded.

"Leave the door open will ya, so I can see when Tad comes in."

She didn't answer, but didn't shut the door behind her.

Robert watched Tad walk in minutes later. Tad sat down the coffees and a bag of biscuits. He walked over to the captain's office and knocked on the door jam.

"Good morning, sir. I brought you a coffee. I don't know how you take it, but there are creams and sugars in the biscuits bag I think. I didn't bring you a biscuit though. I apologize."

"That's ok, Detective. My wife does a good job of feeding me a homemade breakfast before I leave every morning. She'd be offended if she found out I was eating breakfast elsewhere. But, thank you for the coffee." He took the coffee and then gestured toward the chair. "I have to speak with you anyway. Please shut the door and have a seat."

Tad shut the door and sat down. His brows furrowed. "That doesn't sound like good news, Captain. I hope Cap isn't requesting me back. It's only been a couple months..."

"No, your captain hasn't asked for you back. Though I don't know how he's going to feel once he and I talk. I just needed to inform to you first and get your decision before I talk with him."

Tad took a sip of his coffee in anticipation for Captain Armstrong to continue.

"Detective, I received a phone call not too long ago. From William."

"Psycho killer William."

The captain confirmed it with a nod. "The same. He saw you leave Angela's house this morning, and just like I told her, I don't care why you were there. That's not the top priority at the moment. The fact of the matter is that he saw you and called me threatening you for distracting Angela when her focus needs to be on him."

"Threatened how? And how does he know who I am?"

"He doesn't. He did advise me however that that it wouldn't be difficult for him to find out and take you out of the picture."

"Sir, with all due respect, what exactly did he say?"

"That he would carve the words 'No Distractions' into your body much like he carved up that little girl."

Tad sat back in his chair and rubbed his mouth with the back of his hand. He sat without speaking for a few minutes and then said, "I assume you've already advised Angela of this phone call."

"I have."

Tad let out a curse.

"I advised her that I would give you the choice of what you want to do next. You can take leave for the rest of the day. You can choose to go back to your station and let Angela continue the investigation alone. You are also welcome to continue out the day if you'd like and continue on as Angela's partner. It's completely up to you, and I will not judge you on your decision. I am going to call your captain and give him the heads up about the phone call so at the very least, even if you choose to stay, he can add patrol to your house in case William does decide to attempt to make good on his threat."

"Do you think he will?"

"I'm not sure, but I wouldn't want to risk your life even if I believed that he just wanted to spook us. If you need a minute to process this, that's fine. However, I do need to know what you intend to do rather soon so I can go ahead and make that phone call."

Tad put his coffee on the desk in front of him and put his head in his hands. He sighed and then rubbed his hands up and down on his face. He knew what he was going to do, but this phone call was going to push Angela back today. The phone call solidified the fear Angela held. Anyone around her is a target.

"Sir, please tell my captain that I do not and will not waver in my decision to stay on this case with Detective Burns. Part of this job is risk of retaliation from some psycho. Also, I don't want extra patrol around my house. I don't want to put anyone in danger in case he comes prowling around my place. I don't have any roommates or animals at home waiting for me. It's just an empty house. I already have an alarm system and a damn good one. If I need to, I can stay elsewhere or even here at the station if it makes everyone more comfortable. I don't care how we do it. I stated my intentions at the beginning and they haven't changed. Frankly, sir, this piece of shit can kiss my ass. The only thing that has me worried is that Angela won't want me as a partner anymore."

The captain's face remained neutral but internally he smiled. He knew he liked Tad for a reason. Despite Angela's attempts to hide it, Robert watched their looks across the table. Each examining the other while the other wasn't watching. He saw the feelings written all over Tad's face. He would make sure that Angela wasn't going to go through this alone. This started about his partner and family's murder, but now it's about Angela too. He approved of Tad. He was the kind of man her dad and he always wanted for Angela.

"She's expressed concern with your continued involvement now that you're on his radar. But, if you want to continue investigating the case with her, I'm sure she will keep her concerns to herself."

Tad snorted in derision. "Because Angela tends to keep her opinions to herself."

The captain laughed. "I'm sure you can handle it. The fact that you're on this case in the first place despite her feelings about having anyone around her says something about you."

"You're around her, sir."

"That's true but then again I'm her boss so there wasn't any way of getting around it."

"I think it's more than that, sir. I don't mean to pry—"

"You do, but continue."

"I see the relationship between the two of you and the affection you have toward each other. You two attempt to keep a professional boundary at work. However, I've also now been to her house and there are pictures of you two and others who I assume are both of your families. I believe that your relationship goes deeper than captain and detective, sir."

The captain clasped his hands on his desk and debated on how much truth to reveal.

"It's no secret that her father and I were once partners and we all know just how deep some partnerships on the force can bind people together."

Tad nodded in understanding. "That's what I figured, sir. Is there anything else we need to discuss, or can I go back and eat my cold biscuit before Angela and I begin our day?"

"Nothing further, Detective." He looked over into the conference room and saw Angela sitting at the conference table with her coffee in her hands. He'd bet that she hadn't touched that coffee or the biscuit Tad brought her. Her thoughts were on the murder board at home and how much she needed to solve this case before something else happened. "Angela should have the address for the burner phone he used by now. I want you two to pick it up and dust it for prints. Look and ask around and see if anyone saw anything or if any security cameras caught anything."

"Will do, sir. Enjoy the coffee."

Tad walked back into the conference room and pulled both biscuits out of the bag. "Eat. They both somehow aren't cold yet, but they're getting there and we need to go anyway. You fix your coffee yet so I can put the creams and sugars in the break room?"

Angela silently grabbed her coffee and took a sip. She grabbed a cream from the bag and put it in her coffee.

"By the way, I gave your name at the shop because you never said what type of biscuit you wanted. Thankfully, the lady told me that you have a standing order. I told her just make it two. She says hi, by the way."

Angela just nodded her head and took a bite of her biscuit.

"Are you at any point going to talk to me?" Tad waved a hand across her face until she looked up at him. "Well, that's a start."

"You didn't take the out," she finally said in a whisper.

Tad couldn't decide if it was anger or fear edged that her words.

"Nope, I didn't. I told you from the beginning that I would let you know if and when I needed a minute and you agreed to treat me like how a partner should. That still stands. I don't care that I'm on this psycho's radar. It was only a matter of time anyway since I am working this case with you." He finished his biscuit and motioned for her to finish with hers. "We need to get going. Do you have the address?"

She slid over the paper with the address and map on it. He looked at it, but then slid it back to her.

"I have no clue where that is as usual so you'll be driving... as usual."

She finished her biscuit and they headed out. He put the address in his phone's GPS even though he was sure she knew where they were going. He wanted to start knowing his way around the area and the GPS helped him memorize the routes. They ended up at a gas station two streets from her house.

"This isn't close to the shop where I got the biscuits."

"Nope, they're in opposite directions."

"See, I'm not too high on his radar if he didn't even follow me to the shop."

She mumbled a *hmmm* in response and then turned to him. "What can I do to get you to be on garbage duty while I go inside and inquire about the video footage?"

He squinted his eyes and pursed his lips. "You're lucky I like you. Though, I will say for the record that we're right around the corner from your house and you can go and change if you get gross. I don't have that luxury."

She responded with squinted eyes and pursed lips. "I don't appreciate your very valid argument, Detective."

"I knew you wouldn't, but I needed it to be on record." He pulled out rubber gloves and snapped them onto his hands. He got out of the car and headed toward the dumpster while she walked inside.

Angela waited in line until she reached the counter. She flashed her badge and inquired if the guy behind the counter had been working all morning. He acknowledged that he had. She pulled out the age-enhanced photo of William and asked if he'd seen a man fitting this description. The guy shook his head no. She asked if he noticed anyone throwing something away in his dumpster. He denied knowledge and stated that he never paid too much attention to the outside unless there was a commotion, because the mornings are his busy times with everyone trying to get gas and coffee before work. She inquired about security footage. He stated that the only security footage his cheap-ass boss kept was for the front counter. She requested to see the footage from this morning in case the guy she was looking for did come in. She might be able to get a better picture of him than the one she currently had. He told her that he'd call his boss and see what he said. He came back moments later and stated that his boss would be coming in shortly to show her the tapes since he wanted to see her badge and didn't want his staff to leave the front desk. She agreed to wait, and told him that she would go check on her partner while she waited. She turned to leave the store as Tad strolled in with a baggie in hand. He smiled and showed her the burner phone within the bag.

"Thankfully, he just threw it over into the dumpster, so it sat on top of the garbage bags. The hardest part was getting into the dumpster honestly."

"Uhhh... I don't think that's legal to just go through our dumpsters like that," the boy behind the counter commented.

"It's completely legal. Besides, you want to stop us from catching a killer, kid?"

The boy blanched. "No, sir."

"Of course you don't," Tad turned to Angela. "Did you get the tapes?"

"We're waiting for his boss to arrive in order for us to view the tapes. He said—" she motioned with her thumb over to the clerk, "that the boss shouldn't take long. He apparently doesn't live too far from here. Right?" She looked over to the clerk who nodded his head in reply.

They hung around the store for a little bit before the boss came in. He shook their hands and requested to see their badges. Once he saw their credentials, he showed them to his office and pulled up the security cameras. Angela told him that the suspect would have shown up on the camera anytime between seven a.m. and nine a.m. She wanted to view a larger window of time than they needed just in case. The boss put in the timeframe and sat with them as they watched the footage. They fast-forwarded through the lulls and played the footage when someone came to the counter. They didn't see anyone come in that looked like William, but they didn't want to take any chances. Angela requested a copy of the footage so they could go over it again if they needed to. The boss advised that he would send all they had so far from today, since they don't keep anything past forty-eight hours. He didn't want to accidentally delete a timeframe that they may need down the line. Tad and Angela both gave him their thanks. Angela checked her email on her phone to ensure that she received the footage, and they thanked him for his time and cooperation. They headed back to the car and back to the precinct.

They walked into the precinct and the captain waved them into his office. They sat down and closed the door behind them. He asked them how everything went. Tad held up the baggie with the burner phone and Angela reported that they received a copy of the footage from this morning at the gas station. They took a preliminary look with the supervisor and initially didn't see anything. However, they will go over the video again and for more than just the initial time frame.

"Sounds good. Get that down to the lab. Angela, make sure both Tad and I have a copy of the footage please. Tad, I talked to your captain. He wants you to come by the station and go over the plan for security at your house. I advised him of what you told me, but he still wants to talk to you. Since it's going to take time for the lab to get any evidence off the phone, and it's going to take time for you to get back to your precinct, why don't you both go ahead and finish the day from home. We'll reconvene in the morning and go over anything from the footage that might pop up."

They both nodded in agreement and headed home. Tad stopped by his office and spoke with his captain. They agreed that Tad would check in once he got home at night if he went home. Tad refused to allow a patrol car to sit outside his house. The captain advised him that whether he liked it or not, a patrol car would roll by a couple of times a night to check on him at the very least. After they settled terms, they spoke about the case and how the other cases Tad previously had on his load were going with the other detectives.

Once Tad left the department, he decided to make a pit stop before heading home. He turned right from the station and drove to see his best friend. He parked his car next to the patch of grass where he and his family lay. Everyone agreed to just two headstones since the family all laid to rest together. Nick and June shared one headstone while the children shared another. Tad paid extra for their pictures to be put onto the headstones. He knew that seeing their faces on his visits would help, and he didn't want their lives to just amount to a shared piece of stone. They had been so much more than that. Tad pulled out a flattened coin from his pocket and put it next to the glass encased photo of his partner.

"Hey Nick. I'm sorry I haven't been around much since the funeral. I've been working hard with Angela." He looked away from the stone as his voice began to tremble.

"That and it's... uh... it's really hard to be here sometimes, man. I just miss you guys so much." He cleared his throat and changed the subject.

"Angela and I ended up having to go and talk with someone recently. Nothing ended up coming from it, but he worked at the museum. They had one of those stupid coin maker things you loved so much. I had to get one for you. I told Angela all about your love for those things and she just laughed and said that she loves them too. I think you two would have gotten along. She has a lot to learn when it comes to having a partner, but she'll get there. You taught me how to be a good partner, so I'm sure I can teach her just fine. I like her, Nick. I really do. And this of course would be the moment where you make fun of me because of course I would fall for the girl who has an obsessed, psycho killer after her. But that's not the important part right now."

He cleared his throat again. "I'm going to get him for you guys. I promise. I know I make the same promise every time and I haven't made good on it yet, but I promise I will. I'll get you guys justice. Anyway, I just wanted to give you that stupid coin and update you on what's been going on."

He crouched down and rubbed his thumb across both pictures, one after the other. "I miss you guys so much. I'll be back soon. See ya later, alligator."

He rubbed one last time over little Kelly's face and then went back to his place. He made himself a cup of coffee while his laptop booted up. When everything came up, he sat down at his desk, pulled up his email with the footage, and pressed play.

———

Robert studied Angela as she studied the murder board. He took a sip from his sweet tea and wondered how he was going to bring this up. He knew she would reject what he had to say. She would spout nonsense about protecting him or how letting someone else in would cause more liability about everything that they've been keeping a secret. They both knew those reactions would be excuses. He knew she blamed herself for each and every family up on her board. She didn't want Tad to blame her too. She need not worry on that front, he thought to himself. Tad knew who truly was to blame and his opinion wouldn't change upon receiving the full truth. He couldn't help thinking how much Tad and Jackson would have gotten along. Robert wasn't sure if Tad was aware just how far he would go to protect Angela, but Robert had a pretty good idea. He was happy to see someone wanting to take care of his girl the way she took care of everyone else. He just hoped Angela would get out of her own way when all of this was over. They just had to get past William first.

He fought to let her know he had something to say.

"Forget it," she said.

He waited her out.

"Just forget it. He doesn't need to know everything. We can do this without filling him in. You know just as well as I do—"

"That any argument you're going to make will be an excuse. Despite everything, he's stayed on this case. He's lived up to the reputation that he's a good detective and a trustworthy man as far as I'm concerned."

"But that's because he doesn't know everything. That will change if he does." She kept her face glued to the board instead of turning to face him.

"No, it won't. He'll tell you the same thing I've been telling you. You're not the cause of this bastard's obsession and everything he's done."

"Tell that to everyone who stays away because I'm his target," she spat. "But it really doesn't matter does it? I don't really get a say in the matter."

"No," he admitted. "Tad has earned his place on this case, and he can't successfully be your partner without all the facts."

She glared at him. Her nostrils flared with each breath as she tried to keep herself from speaking to both her captain and godfather with disrespect. "Fine, but I believe with all due respect sir that you should have this conversation alone. I don't need to see his face when you fill him in and he decides that he wants to step aside."

"Do you really believe that he's going to decide to leave when he's given this information?" His eyebrow rose in skepticism.

She didn't meet his eye.

"I don't believe you're giving Tad enough credit." His voice softened. "It's not just about justice for his partner anymore. I see the way you two look at each other—"

"Captain, if you want me to be there, I will. But I request not to be there if I don't need to be. If, and that's a big if, he chooses to continue working this case with me, he and I will obviously have a conversation afterwards. If he chooses to transfer back to his precinct, we can skip any awkwardness." Or any looks of loathing while my heart breaks, she thought to herself.

"I will have the discussion with him and stress the understanding of the discretion as well no matter which way he decides."

"I want it noted this is a mistake."

"I don't believe it is."

Angela gazed at him and then turned back to the murder board. "When are you having this discussion?"

"Tomorrow."

She nodded. "I assume not at the station."

"No, not at the station. I will request for him to meet me at my house as an added precaution that no one overhears and we can't be interrupted."

"I'll focus on paperwork until I get an update from you."

"Work from home and I'll send him to you after."

"Understood."

He put his arm around her shoulders and shook her gently. She smiled like he knew she would.

"We're going to catch him, Angela." He stared at the murder board with her and wondered just how many more families would die before they did.

15

Alexander stared at the Jones' house from a few doors down. According to the shadows at the blinds, the family gathered together in the formal dining room. He looked at the time on his dash. 6:15. *Prompt family dinner time,* he thought to himself. He pressed the numbers on his burner phone and put it up to his ear. It rang once to connect and then he heard the familiar greeting:

"911. What's your emergency?"

"Help! There is someone in my house! I think he has a gun! Someone needs to get here now!" He faked panic in his voice as he gave the neighbor's address two doors down from the Jones' home. "Oh my God! He's coming!"

He ended the call with a click, not giving the operator a moment to respond. 911 always called back but he never answered. He noted the time on the dash once again and waited for the sirens. Ten minutes later, two cop cars blared their sirens as they sped past him. Ten minutes didn't give him enough time to get in and get out of the family's home, so he made a note in his journal that he needed to call afterwards. He didn't like the family to sit too long afterwards, and baby sister had a long drive ahead of her after all.

16

Tad pulled up to Captain Armstrong's house. He didn't understand why the captain wanted to meet here. He got out of the car and waved. The captain stood at the already open door. He greeted Tad and advised that he saw the car pull up on his security system. He asked Tad if he wanted a cup of coffee and Tad stated that he didn't. The captain introduced Tad to his wife before leading him into a closed off office space upstairs away from all the bedrooms. The captain sat behind his desk and Tad sat across from him.

"You have a nice house, sir. But, I must confess I don't understand why we're meeting here. There is a perfectly good desk in your office that you can sit behind and me in front of."

"There aren't prying eyes and a chance of being overheard here."

Instead of answering, Tad waited for him to continue.

"Yesterday, you asked me if my relationship with Angela goes deeper than captain and detective."

"And you confirmed my suspicion without actually confirming."

"I did. But, I intend to do more this morning. You've been Angela's partner on this case and have proven that you're a man who can handle all facets of this case."

"Whereas I couldn't before?"

"Certain details involving this case needed to be kept close to the vest. You made a good argument to get on this case in the beginning, but there was no way to know if you would continue throughout the life of this case. However, I believe that since you're now on William's radar and you're choosing to continue on as partner, you deserve all of the details regarding this case. There is one caveat though, and I need you to understand the severity of this. This does not go beyond the three of us. Ever. Whether this goes to trial or whether William ends up in the ground, certain details don't ever need to come to light."

"You're asking me to essentially break the law aren't you, sir." This wasn't a question.

"I'm saying that we will have enough evidence to catch and convict the guy without this information. But, if it makes you uncomfortable, we can stop this conversation now."

Tad leaned back in his chair and laced his fingers together in front of him on his stomach. "I don't care what I gotta do to catch this guy. He took my family."

"Is that the only reason?"

"Sir, you got to where you are for a reason, and I'm sure you're well aware of my feelings for Angela."

"I am. I just wonder how aware you are regarding them."

"I'm one hundred percent self-aware. It's Angela that isn't."

The captain smiled. "Oh, I believe she's just as aware and that's her problem."

"For the record, my feelings don't get in the way of the main goal of catching this psycho. I'll convince Angela that we're meant to be together afterwards, but right now, our focus is on the case."

"If I thought any differently, you wouldn't stay on this case."

"Understood. Now, what are the details about this case that I'm missing?"

"I'm getting there. I'll start at the beginning, and you can hold any questions or comments until the end."

Then the captain began to talk. He told Tad everything: from his relationship to Angela, Angela's father, William's identity, down to the fabricated detail regarding the fingerprint. Tad sat in silence. He barely blinked. When the captain finished, he waited for some sort of reaction out of Tad. He didn't know what to expect exactly. He expected some questions or some sort of reaction maybe, but Tad just sat there processing the information in utter silence. Finally, Tad spoke.

"Ok."

"Ok?"

"Ok." Tad rubbed his face with his hands. "I mean, that pretty much connects all the dots I had dangling in my head. Though, I never would have guessed this in a million years.

God, no wonder why you two kept this a secret. I don't know why you even let me on this case in the first place."

"Because you reminded me of Jackson."

Tad just stopped. He understood the gravity of that sentence after all the conversations with Angela regarding her father. "Thank you, sir. I appreciate you providing me with all of the details, and I will not share this information."

"Good. Let's not make me regret this."

Tad tilted his head and thought for a moment. "She didn't want you to tell me, did she?"

The captain didn't respond.

"She didn't want you to tell me because she incorrectly assumes that I will blame her the way she blames herself."

The captain once again didn't respond, but Tad continued.

"I always knew she blamed herself, but it makes so much more sense now."

"She's working from home today. You'll have to call her though. She won't hear you knocking while she's in the basement. Dismissed."

Tad nodded his head and left the captain's home.

———

Tad arrived at Angela's house. He'd already texted her that he was on his way, so she met him at the door. She ushered him inside and led him to the kitchen table where they sat across from each other. On the table sat a composition book. The binding was duct taped and fragile. The design on the cover was worn with age. She slid the notebook over to him. He opened the cover and saw the date at the top.

"I know Cap gave you all the details except this one. He knows about it, but he also knows that it's my decision to show it to you. It's my biological father's notebook. William sent it to me after I found out about him. I don't know how he knew, but I found it on my doorstep within a few days of being told he was my half sibling. Stephen was already gone by that point so the only people who know are the captain, me, and now you. Well, Mother knew but she's gone now. I took it to her after I received it and she confirmed that it was his. She begged me not to read it, but I did it anyway. Mother didn't originally give me details about what she found in my father's journals." She tapped her fingers on the book. "I got all I wanted and more in there. It took months for me to get through it. I kept having to stop because—"

"You don't have to explain."

"You need to understand. I know the captain gave you the details but I need you to truly understand. You know he's my half-brother now and you know he has an end game with me. But I doubt he told you where or how it started. He came up with all of this because of our father. My biological father wanted to kill me. Had to physically stop himself from killing me as a baby. My twisted brother found this journal, and all the other ones I'm sure were left behind, and is determined to finish what our father started. That's what you're walking into. That's why I have worked this case alone. That's why I am alone. It's not safe. I know you say there is a certain level of risk with this job, but it's not the same as the level of risk you face here. You can walk away and I won't blame you. I know you want justice for Nick and June and the kids, but I can do that alone. I swear to you that I'll do that. You can walk away."

He looked at her from across the table. "You're waiting for me to condemn you for your brother's actions. You're waiting for me to blame you for Nick and June and the kids."

He got up from the table. He got down on his knees in front of her and cupped her face in his hands.

"I need you to hear me. Your twisted father isn't your fault. Your twisted brother isn't your fault. Your ex—whoever the fuck he was—is not me. He couldn't handle it but I can. We'll have time for that particular talk after everything is settled, but that's not the point right now. The point right now is catching this killer. Us... we'll just keep doing whatever 'us' is right now and label it later."

He kissed her then. He kissed her with all the passion and assurances that only he could provide. Angela relished in the moment. He didn't hate her. He didn't condemn her. No matter what happened with William at the end of this, she had this moment with Tad and all the little moments they've been sharing. She'd been ready for the death match for so long, but now she wanted more of this. Would fight for more of this. His lips left hers. He whispered kisses on her eyelids before resting his forehead against hers.

"Now that we've settled that, I'm sure the captain is going to want us to come into work."

"Actually, we can work from here. We couldn't before because you were in the dark about certain things, but now we can work from my murder board. It's more extensive anyway."

"In the basement, right? It makes sense now why the captain told me to text you since you would be in the basement and wouldn't hear me."

"Yep. I'll check in really quick and get the go-ahead. I'm certain we'll be able to work from here when we're not in the field since it's what I previously did before you came along."

"Though I may need to be more discrete about my car moving forward."

"That's true. I can just have you park out back instead of in the driveway. That door right there," she pointed to the door behind her, "leads to the back deck and you can just come and go from it. We'll keep a watch out for any cars or people around when you leave so if he sees you leave again hopefully we will have clocked his presence."

"Seems like a decent enough plan. Or I can leave my car at the station and just ride with you to and from here. That way he only sees one car."

"And what happens when you need to go home?"

"I can pack a bag and stay here." He wiggled his eyebrows.

She chuckled. "Slow your roll there, cowboy. Just because we kissed doesn't mean I want you to move in."

"I don't know.... I do make pretty good company."

She rolled her eyes. He gave into temptation and pulled her into his embrace. He covered her mouth with his. One hand roamed from her hips up to her neck as he deepened the kiss. The other moved to cup her breast over her shirt. She moaned in response. He moved his kisses from her lips to her neck as he began unbuttoning her shirt. His mouth met the top of her bra and he tugged the laced fabric aside. His tongue licked across her nipple. Her fingers wove themselves into his hair as she gasped.

"That's it, honey," he whispered.

Her hands found the front of his pants. She slid her palm across his bulge. He nipped gently at her breast.

A loud buzzing vibrated the table in front of her.

"Of course..." he sighed into her cleavage. "Go ahead. I'm sure it's work."

She checked the phone's called ID and saw the lab's number flash across the screen. She picked it up and listened to the other end. She stated her understanding and thanks before she hung up the phone.

"That was the lab. Just like we expected, no prints on the phone. I confess that I didn't rewatch the video footage last night. Did you?"

"I did, but I don't mind going over it again with you. It obviously was late, and it never hurts to go over things again and again. We have no other leads."

"No, but we need to drive around the area near the gas station and look for other cameras. If we're lucky, maybe we can catch a traffic light camera or something."

"You don't know your own neighborhood well enough to know where the cameras are?" he teased.

"Oh, and you do?" She raised one eyebrow and leaned forward to rest her jaw in her palm.

"Of course I do. Nick demanded it. He thought it helpful to know where all the cameras are so that way we don't have to do what we're about to do when we're looking for leads on a case. Saves time."

A small smile softened her face. "Nick really was a great detective, wasn't he?"

"He really was. He was great at everything honestly. He went one-hundred percent into everything he did."

"But June wasn't like that was she? Based on all those stories you told me."

A sad smile crept onto his face. "No, she wasn't. He used to call her his roots because she kept him grounded." He chuckled. "I don't know how his nickname for her never came up in our talks since he called her that so often. She was the roots for Kelly too. I told you before, that girl inherited his balls-to-the-wall mentality."

"What about David? What was he like? You've mentioned him some but not as much as the others."

He thought for a moment. "A good mix between the two. Quiet like June. Loved his video games as most boys his age do. But, he had drive like his dad. When he loved something, he spent hours researching it and he talked about it with such vigor. Nick and June never really understood video games and they didn't play with him because they were terrible.

But, they listened to him talk about it. They always made him feel heard and supported. For his last birthday, they took him to one of those gaming places. They didn't have fun, but David and I sure did."

"They sound wonderful."

"Obviously, they weren't perfect. But, yeah, they were."

She reached across the table and squeezed his hand gently.

Tad sighed. "Let's go look at the video footage again. Got any popcorn or snacks? I like to snack when going over video footage."

"Who doesn't? I have a locker full of snacks and a fridge full of soda in the basement where my laptop and everything is."

"You are the perfect woman," Tad said.

He gave her a quick peck on the lips before following her to the basement. Tad pulled out snacks and two sodas for them as they sat down to watch the tapes.

———

Hours later, they emerged from the basement, no closer to any answers. Angela called the captain and advised that they did not obtain any further information from the footage. Captain advised that he didn't find anything either when he reviewed it from his office computer. He then asked her to go into another room without Tad so he could ask her a question and she could answer without issue. She decided not to joke and tell him he wasn't on speakerphone because she could hear the seriousness in his tone that he normally reserved for his daughters that were just reaching their teen years. She excused herself to the back deck and advised that she could speak freely. Captain asked her how her talk went with Tad. She told him that it went how he expected, and she thanked him for having more faith than her about Tad, because he was right. She advised him that she and Tad would spend the next day searching around the area for any other cameras that might be able to give them anything since it was almost quitting time. The captain agreed and ended the call.

"So, dinner?" Tad asked.

"I was thinking about ordering in. How does that sound?" Angela replied.

"Works for me. What you in the mood for?"

"Hmmm... pizza?"

"Eh... I had that the other night. Chinese?"

"I could go for Chinese food."

Angela picked up the Chinese food menu from her menu drawer and handed it to Tad. Tad picked out what he wanted and Angela ordered it along with her usual. She pulled out her debit card, but Tad plucked it out of her hand and replaced it with his. She went to argue with him but he just put a finger to his lips. She rolled her eyes and paid with his card.

"You know I'm capable of paying every once in a while, right? You're the one spending all this money on gas to drive here every day to work this case. The least I can do is pay."

"You must be confusing me with someone who isn't a Southern gentleman who would never allow a lady to pay." He flashed her his 100 Watt smile that somehow hadn't gotten old yet, despite them working so closely over these past couple of months, and wiggled his eyebrows.

"This lady is your partner." She stared him down with her hands on her hips.

"Yes, you are, and you can pay for coffee and such when we're on the clock if you're so inclined. But, we're off the clock at the moment, so that just makes us a man and a woman having dinner together, and therefore, the woman does not pay."

She rolled her eyes but couldn't help laughing. "Next you'll be telling me that you're in charge of the remote since you're the man."

"Oh no ma'am." He poured out his most potent Southern accent. "Us Southern boys always let the lady decide the movie. It's only polite."

She glared at him. "If you don't quit, I will make you watch a cheesy romantic movie full of clichés."

"Oh, but I bet you wouldn't, Angela Burns. You strike me as the horror and thriller genre kind of girl who absolutely despises romantic movies. You would be punishing yourself." He sat down on the couch and made himself comfortable with his feet laid out in front of him on the chaise portion of her couch.

"Keep going and I'll punish myself just to punish you," she laughed despite her determination not to.

She sat down next to him with her feet curled underneath her. Her head leaned on his shoulder as she turned on the TV and put on her favorite old school thriller. Once the food arrived, they ate and laughed at all the incorrect police work in the film. After the movie, Tad looked at his watch and groaned.

"I better get going before it gets too late. Rush hour has ended but soon it'll be where I'm getting home late, and I got to drive back up here early so we can look for any cameras."

"Or you can stay here tonight if you'd like. Tomorrow is Friday, so you can just drive home tomorrow and avoid all the back and forth." She began to unbutton his shirt. "I could just put your clothes in the wash like last time."

He fisted his hand in her hair at the nape of her neck. Her lips trailed her fingers down the length of his chest. She untucked his button-down and undershirt before sliding her hand underneath to touch his skin. His skin felt hot under her touch. She leaned in, her lips a whisper away from his.

"You didn't answer me."

He pulled her mouth to his. His fist tightening as he deepened the kiss. His other hand wrapped itself around her waist and pulled her body closer against his. His hand left her hair so both hands could cup her bottom. Her legs were now straddling his lap. She broke the kiss long enough to pull his shirts over his head. She needed to feel his skin again. He unbuttoned her shirt and she slid it off her body. His hands cupped her breasts as he pulled down the strap of her bra. His kisses trailed from her mouth to her nipple. She gasped as he gently sucked. Her fingers pulled his hair and she let out a moan of pleasure. He pulled his mouth away and she felt the sudden cold from where the heat of his mouth just been.

"As much as I just want to continue this here on the couch, I do believe we need to move this to the bedroom. It'd be more comfortable." He whispered against her neck. His fingers continuing to rub against her nipple and rob any other thought from her mind.

He nipped at her earlobe to regain her attention. "Honey, which way to the bedroom again?"

"Just past the kitchen."

His mouth found hers again as he lifted her in his arms. Her legs straddled him. His lips lefts hers so he could find the bedroom. She took advantage of this by nibbling on his ear. She took off her bra and they were skin to skin. It took everything he had to get them to the bedroom. He kicked the door closed before they fell onto the bed.

17

Alexander waited in his car until all the lights were off in the house and it sat quiet for at least an hour. The father would be easier to subdue if woken versus catching him alert just after finishing up reading legal documents in his office. He checked the time on his dashboard: 12:36 AM. He pulled out the knife he had swiped from the daughter and twirled it in his already gloved fingers. He wondered if she knew it was missing yet. He looked at the neighbors' homes. Their lights went out hours ago, but he watched the windows in each neighbor's house around the cul-de-sac while he waited in his car to ensure no movement caught his eye. Sometimes people need a midnight snack or their bladder wakes them up demanding release. Nobody wants to turn on the lights for that. He stretched his neck. 12:40 glowed on the dash. Time to go.

He opened up the car door and hit the automatic lock on the interior of the driver side door so the lock wouldn't chirp and alert anyone to his presence. He stashed the car key in his bottom left cargo pocket for a quick getaway. He jogged across the road. Using the shadows of each house to cover him, he moved to the Jones' home. He reached the house and snuck around to the back deck. He hoped they hadn't caught his tampering with the back door in the couple of days since he'd done his walk through. He assumed they were the type of family to come in through either the front or garage door. He picked the lock and opened the door slowly. No alarm sound. He closed his eyes and sighed. He walked over to the door that led to the garage and locked it. He didn't want them fleeing to the car—not that they ever get the chance to flee—but he didn't want to leave any stone unturned. He moved through the kitchen and formal dining room into the living room, then checked the front door to make sure it was locked. He smiled to himself. Looks like one of the residents, likely the father since he tends to be the last one to bed, forgot to latch the chain lock above the deadbolt. Alex turned his head to the side. He didn't remember that chain lock when he was here the other day. *Seems a little paranoid in a nice neighborhood like this one.* He slid the chain to lock it, careful not to let it rattle against the door. He turned to look at the stairs. Fourteen steps. He remembered a few steps had creaks: two, three, four, and twelve. His grandma always screamed at him for not having foresight growing up. If she wasn't already dead, he might have called her up to thank her for screaming the notion of foresight into his head all those years ago. He maneuvered up the stairs careful to step to the side of the steps that creaked. He turned and snuck to the son's room.

The door was closed and the light was turned off. He kneeled onto the carpet and pulled a mirror from his pocket. It didn't hurt to double check for any movement in the bedroom since he didn't want the son to alert the rest of the family. He pushed the mirror under the doorframe and tilted it so he could view into the room. He moved it side to side so he could check the whole room. No movement. He opened the door slowly then made his way to the bed. The son lay asleep facing away from him. Alexander watched the comforter rise and fall with each breath. He pulled out the knife and held it tightly in his hand. He hoped the son enjoyed nice images for his last dream. He swooped his hand under the son's neck and wrapped his palm over his mouth as he pulled him to a sitting position. He dug the knife into the side of his neck. The son's eyes popped open as he pulled the knife out and Alexander watched the spray of blood coat everything in its path with every heartbeat. He counted the seconds in his head as the spray died down. He laid him back onto the bed and pulled the covers up to his neck, covering the wound. He turned from the bed and walked out of the son's bedroom. Next up, the daughter's room.

He cocked his head to the side and listened for a moment. Silence. He smiled to himself before walking to the daughter's room. He once again kneeled onto the carpet and pulled a mirror from his pocket. He pushed the mirror under the doorframe and tilted it to peer into the bedroom. No movement. He saw a mountain of covers on the bed bundled together as if a person was asleep under the sheets, but he suspected the daughter wasn't underneath the blankets. How could he have missed her sneaking out? He cursed inwardly.

Of course she would throw off his plans. The girl with her own priorities that her parents would never approve of. He turned the doorknob slowly and opened the door to ensure no creaking, just in case he was wrong about the lump of covers on the bed. She might sleep like a mole person, who knows? He stayed crouched so if she came through the window she wouldn't see any movement while climbing back into her room. He pushed down on the center of the covers to test for resistance. Just as he suspected, his hand pushed into a soft pillow. He pulled the sheets back and found two pillows shaped to look like her body. He thought it seemed a bit cliché to sneak out and leave that behind, but it seemed to work. He sat on the bed and scratched at his eyebrow with the unsharpened side of the knife. The son's blood coated the brow. He moved his head toward his shoulder—right to left, right to left—to loosen the muscles underneath while he thought of what to do next. Who knew when the girl would be home. He saw a shadow move out of the corner of his eye. Alexander smiled. *Perfect timing.* He crouched down as he made his way to over to the window, making sure to stay in the shadows so she wouldn't see him. She slowly opened the window and climbed in. She only put the tips of her feet to the floor and added her weight gradually so the floorboard wouldn't creak. She turned back to put the alarm wires back together when she felt the knife against her throat.

"Don't scream, Sophie."

Her breath hitched, but she did what he said. Alexander pulled a zip tie from his pocket and turned her to face him.

"Put your hands together and do as I say."

She did as he asked once again, but instead of questions or crying, she stared at him with fire in her eyes. He found himself thinking once more just how much he liked this girl.

"I'm going to have to use both hands to tie you up. If you attempt anything, I'm going to gut you like a deer. Do we have an understanding?"

She didn't reply. He took that as consent. She didn't move as he wrapped her wrists together with the zip tie. He put the knife back to her throat and stepped behind her so her body shielded his from the front.

"Now, let's go see your parents," he whispered close to her ear as he pushed her forward.

That earned him a turn around from her. She didn't even flinch as the shallow cut from her head turn caused tiny droplets of blood. She narrowed her eyes in a glare. He pushed the tip of the knife up into the soft skin of her throat behind her jawbone and tsked at her. She turned her head back around and he pushed her forward a second time, out of her room and down the hallway. She glanced at her brother's closed door as they walked past it. Alexander thought about leaning forward and whispering how she didn't have to worry about her older brother but he decided against it. This one would fight him given any opportunity and right now she was doing as he said. They reached the doors of the parents' bedroom.

"Careful now," he warned her.

They opened the door and Alexander turned on the light. The parents rolled over and covered their faces with their hands before questioning who turned on the lights. Mrs. Jones removed her hands from her eyes first and sat up straight in the bed when she saw Sophie in the doorway with a knife at her throat. She let out a gasp before the tears fell from her eyes.

"What the fuck?" Mr. Jones yelled.

"What do you want?" Mrs. Jones finally managed to ask.

The father reached into his nightstand and pulled out the gun. Alexander smiled.

"Go ahead. Pull the trigger," he taunted.

The father's hand shook as he lifted the gun to where Alexander and Sophie stood.

"Pull it. Pull it back and listen to the click of an empty chamber."

The father's eyes widened and his mouth opened in shock.

"What do you want?" the mother questioned again.

Alexander turned his attention to the mother.

"I want you both to get up and walk down to the dining room." He turned Sophie so the parents could move around them.

The father kept his eyes trained on Alexander. The mother couldn't break her gaze away from Sophie's.

"It's going to be okay, baby," the mother said trying to console her daughter.

Alexander learned into Sophie's ear, still keeping eye contact with Mr. Jones.

"No, Sophie, it won't."

"Go fuck yourself," Sophie spat back.

Alexander just lifted his eyebrow in response.

Once the parents walked out of the bedroom, Alexander led Sophie down the hallway after them.

They walked down the stairs and into the dining room.

"Noah... where is Noah?" the mother asked.

Alexander ignored her. No sense in making them hysterical before everyone is tied up. That would take longer and he had a schedule to keep. He pulled out two large zip ties out of his pocket and threw them at the mother. She fumbled one before grabbing onto it.

"Tie him up. Tie his wrists to the chair. That chair right there. Make sure it's nice and tight, because I'll check," he pointed to the head of the table. The mother stood there unmoving. Alexander mentally shook his head. *This always happens.*

"Now!"

Mrs. Jones jumped at his anger. She shuffled over to Mr. Jones as he sat down in the chair. Her hands quivered as she wrapped the zip tie around her husband's wrist and pulled.

"Remember what I said now. Nice and tight now. You wouldn't want me to slit your little Sophie's throat because you couldn't follow orders now would you?"

Mrs. Jones shook her head that she understood and cinched it tight enough that Mr. Jones winced.

"Now take the other one and do the same thing with that armrest," Alexander instructed.

She shook her head again in understanding and repeated the process with the other arm. Alexander kept the blade against Sophie's neck as he leaned down to test the zip tie. If it would have mattered soon, Alexander might have been worried about the lack of circulation to Mr. Jones' hands from how tight Mrs. Jones made them. He imagine how painful it must be to have the hard plastic bite into the skin. When he was satisfied, he pulled out two more zip ties and handed them to Sophie.

"Now, Sophie, my dear, I'm going to take this knife off your throat so I can take off your zip tie. Tie your mother up to that chair next to your father. But, if you try anything, I'm going to stab you and make your parents watch you bleed out slowly. Do you understand?"

Sophie just cut her eyes at Alexander and stared at him through her narrowed gaze. Alexander laughed and motioned for her to go ahead once he'd cut the plastic off her. Sophie repeated the process her mother took with her father. The mother just kept blubbering and trying to console Sophie even though Sophie's face remained dry. All that seeped out of her eyes was loathing. Once Sophie completed her task, Alexander instructed her to sit down at the other end of the table and he repeated the process. He pulled out three pieces of cloth from his pocket and tied a piece over each mouth. He didn't want the neighbors to hear them scream. He'd learned a long time ago that you can threaten all you want but once the intended victim figures out that they aren't getting out alive, they scream as loud as they can because they have nothing left to lose but the hope that someone will help them before it's too late.

Now comes the fun part.

"Everyone nice and comfortable?" He paused for a moment as if expecting a response. "Good. Now, to answer your earlier question Mrs. Jones... your son is upstairs in his bed devoid of blood."

Alexander soaked in the mother's reaction like a child soaking in the sun on the first day of summer vacation.

He turned his attention over to the father. "Even with all your locks and protections, you still came up short."

Tears ran down the father's face. Alexander turned his attention back to the mother. He sliced the knife across her skin from the crook of her elbow to her wrist. Blood poured from the gash. Her cries fought against the cloth between her teeth. The father roared and fought against the restraints holding his arms to the chair trying to get to his wife. Sophie just stared at her lap. Tears fell for the first time and made tiny spots on her jeans. Her wrists chafed against the plastic. She jerked her wrists up against the armrest. To her surprise, the armrest came up and separated from the wooden piece attached to the seat of the chair. She pulled up again. She moved her wrist forward to test whether she could slide her tied wrist down the wood. The plastic tie slid without issue. She cut her eyes to Alexander while she slid her wrist forward until she pulled it free. She placed her arm back against the chair so it wouldn't be noticed at first glance. Another tear fell as her gaze moved from Alexander to her mother. She saw the knife running across her mother's other arm, over and over. Little cuts overlapping. Skin beginning to flap from barely being attached anymore. Sophie looked down and saw red carpet instead of the white carpet her mother loved. Her mother will spend hours with a scrubber and hydrogen peroxide trying to change it back to white. Even if she gets it white enough that no one else would ever notice the difference, they will still never hear the end of it. How her pristine white carpet was sullied by a stain. She looked up at her mother's face. Her normally tanned skin that took three to five days a week at the tanning bed to pull off looked muted. Tears still fell from her mother's eyes but now she could barely hold her head up and she wasn't fighting against the cuts anymore. Alexander's attention was focused on the mother so Sophie slowly moved her right arm to her left and wiggled the connector piece until she was sure it would separate if she pulled up. She pulled up with her left arm and it separated enough for her to get her arm free. She tried to meet her father's eyes but he maintained focus on her mother and screamed through the cloth for her to stay awake. She had to go now.

Sophie pushed back the chair and sprinted as fast as her sneakers would take her. Alexander darted to stop her but she shoved her hands against his chest and pushed him against the dining room table. She ran to the front door and turned the knob but the door wouldn't open. She undid the lock and the deadbolt and turned the knob again. This time it only gave way just a little bit before stopping. She yanked on the knob but it wouldn't move. A cry of frustration escaped against the cloth still tied behind her head. She looked up and saw the chain lock her dad installed in response to Noah picking the door lock after staying out past curfew the other night. Her hands shook as she reached toward the knob on the chain to slide it down the track. She unlocked the chain and pulled on the door knob once again. A hand reached over her shoulder and pushed the door back closed with a click. Goosebumps ran down her back as she felt his breath against her ear. He tsked at her softly. His fingers gripped the nape of her hair and shoved her face against the wood. She heard the crunch of her nose and pain exploded her senses. Blood gushed down her lips and chin, soaking the cloth between her teeth. Her tongue touched the fabric and she tasted pennies. Alexander drug her by the nape of her hair across the living room floor and back into the dining room. Her father continued to fight against the restraints and Alexander was able to make out the words muffled and unpronounceable being yelled from behind the cloth. Leave her alone. Alexander pulled Sophie up by her hair and stood her next to her mother in front of her father. He turned her head with his thumb and forefinger. She pushed against his fingers so hard that he left finger marks on her jaw.

"Say goodbye to Mommy, Sophie." Sophie's chest heaved with sobs. Her mother's chest no longer moved with her breath.

He turned her back to face her father. "Now, say goodbye to Daddy, Sophie."

He turned her to face him. "No one could protect you. Not your mother. Not your father. Not even yourself."

Sophie's knees gave out and she tried to fall to the floor. He pulled hard on her hair and she found her footing against the pain. She gave one last attempt and kicked her foot out at his shin. But he let go of her hair long enough to grab her leg mid-kick. He drove the knife into her thigh muscle. Her muffled scream ripped from her body.

"I said you. can't. protect. yourself." Each word punctuated by another stab to the leg. Sophie's body jerked with each thrust.

He let her go and she fell to the floor, cradling her now useless leg. He crouched in front of her and held the knife to her face. "Fire. Always full of fire."

He turned his attention to the father. "Are you watching?"

He laughed as the father continued to fight in his chair. Alexander watched blood begin to drip from the plastic digging into wrists. He moved to crouch behind Sophie. He placed the knife slowly behind her back. He lifted up the back of her shirt and ran his finger down her spine until he found the spot he wanted. He pushed the knife into her spinal column.

"Can't kick me now," he whispered into her ear. "I'll be back!" He exclaimed loud enough for both to hear.

Mr. Jones and Sophie heard doors open and shut in the kitchen. Alexander walked back in with a plastic grocery bag. Sophie shook her head to try and fight against the bag as Alexander put it over her face. Mr. Jones pulled against the zip ties with such force that his chair fell to the side. Alexander tied the bag behind her neck. Then grabbed her arms and pulled them behind her. He looped another zip tie between her already bound wrists before picking up the father's chair from its side. The chair shook with Mr. Jones' sobs.

"Now you." He put Sophie's knife on the table in front of Mr. Jones. "The father who couldn't even protect his family. Like all the others who just didn't have the guts." He unfolded a knife from his pocket almost twice the size of Sophie's. The kind of knife a hunter might use to field dress his murdered prize.

"Your daughter's knife worked well for your son, wife, and even Sophie herself; but it just won't hit deep enough for you."

The father's eyes never faced Alexander as he spoke. His attention stayed on his daughter's face through the bag as she attempted to suck in air that no longer existed. Alexander grabbed the father's chin and forced his focus back to him. Clear lines streaked the father's cheeks. His eyes stared back without seeing. They didn't dart away in fear and they didn't hold fire anymore like Sophie's up until the end. They were the eyes of a man with nothing left to lose. Alexander pushed the knife into his stomach. Mr. Jones hissed behind the cloth. Alexander pulled the knife to the right splitting open the stomach. He thrust the knife in a few more times before he reached inside and pulled the intestines out of the slit. With the blood still coating his gloved hands, he wrote a word and his signature "A" on the white plate setting on the table in front of the father. He stood for a moment, taking in the sight before him. He wanted the mental picture in his mind for later when he recreated the scene on the page. He stared as the bag at Sophie's mouth moved slower and slower. He didn't need to wait for it to stop. According to his test run, they won't make it in time to save her. They'll try, of course, to resuscitate her; but, what the movies don't tell you is that it only works forty percent of the time, and only ten to twenty percent live long enough to get discharged from the hospital. That's not taking into account the stab wound, paralyzing her and bleeding out on the carpet underneath her.

He picked up Sophie's knife from the table and dropped it next to her. He ran the dull side of his knife down his tongue. His eyes rolled back and a small moan left his lips. He folded the knife and put it back in his pocket before walking out the same way he came. He made sure to take down the two cameras he didn't need anymore and remove any evidence they were ever there in the first place. He checked his surroundings as he made his way back to his car. No lights shined from the neighbor's windows. No movement behind the closed curtains. He unlocked the door and removed his gloves. He stuffed the gloves into his pocket and opened up his glove box. He pulled out one of the flip phones he bought from one of the local Walmarts and turned it on. He punched in 911 and brought the phone to his ear. He listened for dispatch's voice on the other line as she repeated the standard greeting.

"Yes ma'am." He never forgot his manners. "I'd like to report a murder. Well, murders." He rattled off the family's address then hung up the phone.

He rolled down the car's passenger side window and threw the phone out of it. He pulled down the sun visor and checked his face in the mirror. A streak of blood stained one eyebrow. Other than that, no trace of blood gave him away. He licked his thumb and rubbed away the blood on his face. He shut the visor and turned on his car, put it in gear, and headed toward the hotel.

When he reached the hotel, he parked his car by the main office. A new face barely looked up from her book long enough to give him a wave from the desk. He gave a small smile as he walked past the office to his hotel room. He'd wash his clothes at the local laundromat later. He buried his clothing in his gym bag of dirty clothing. He always washed everything, gym bag included, in one load and he always made sure to wash it twice. A lady at the laundromat trying to make conversation once asked him why he washed twice. He replied that he didn't feel like these washers ever got his work-out clothing clean enough on the first try.

After his shower, he sat down at the little table and used the remote to turn on the news. He then opened up his journal to the next empty page. He turned his wrist and checked the time. At the very least, baby sister should be awake and headed to the house by now. Just in time for the morning news: Captain Armstrong will stand in front of the station for another press conference and give the same speech he gave at all the press conferences before. He picked up the pen and began to write the events of the evening while he waited for the news to break regarding the Jones family.

18

Angela's cell phone screen lit up on her nightstand. The captain's face and phone number stared back at her through her squinted eyes. She slid her finger across the glass and put the phone to her ear.

"Captain, you couldn't give me my last couple of hours of sleep?" She teased. "I already get up earlier than most."

"No, I couldn't. It seems he struck again last night."

She sat up. Tad rolled over so he faced her with his forearm covering his eyes. He opened his mouth to speak but she clamped her hand over his mouth. "Captain, that's not the timeline. It can't be him. They must have gotten it wrong."

"The same city? He's never struck the same city twice, let alone the same city consecutively. It's not him. They're wrong." She paused again for his response. "Text me the address." She hung up the phone and got up from the bed.

"What's up?" Tad asked while rubbing sleep from his eyes.

"Your local police called Cap and said William struck again."

This time it was Tad's turn to sit up with questions. Angela held up her hand to stop him. "We need to go. I'll brief you on the way. You'll drive separately."

"No need. I've kept my captain up to date on when I won't be home so he doesn't send a patrol car to drive-by my place. And before you freak out, he's been told it's so we can dedicate more time to the case."

Angela gave him a look but didn't reply.

———

They reached the house and parked two doors down like she always did. She told Tad to get out of the car. He watched her place her head against the top of the steering wheel and take three deep breaths. He wasn't sure what to do, so he just turned around, looked toward the crime scene, and he waited. Inside the car, she felt weird completing her ritual, but it felt too wrong not to do it. She needed to prepare herself for the scene, especially since she'd have Tad there for his first walkthrough with her. He turned and watched her step out of the car once he heard the door open and they walked together to the police tape surrounding the house. The same uniform that met her at the last scene wordlessly pushed up the tape so they could walk underneath. Both captains stood in the lawn near the front door talking together. Their conversation ceased as the two walked up to them. They all shook hands and gave greetings. Captain Armstrong spoke first.

"Angela, you go on in and determine if they're right, that this is William. If so, we have a new pattern. Tad, you stay here. If it is him, you can examine the scene with Angela afterwards. Everyone has been ordered out of the house until you've examined the scene."

Angela nodded her head in acknowledgement. Both captains watched Tad's jaw clench with the order, but he didn't buck it. Tad watched Angela turn and walk through the door without him.

"If this is him, why change his pattern now?" Tad asked.

Both captains looked at him but Captain Archer answered. "He hit us twice and he knew about you working this case with her."

Tad's jaw clenched and he looked away.

Captain Armstrong sighed before chiming in. "We all know it's not your fault. If it wasn't this family now, it would be another family in two months unfortunately. And this could afford us new information. Right now, he's mad. He's breaking his pattern. And now we know he's watching her more closely than we realized. This is when he'll make a mistake."

"Maybe," Tad responded, his attention on the front door.

A few more minutes went by before Angela re-emerged through the door. Tad didn't need the answer she was about to give their superiors. The blush that normally colored her cheeks fell away to pallor. Her right hand held a slight tremor. She had pushed her shoulders back in fake strength. When she looked in his eyes and he saw the pain etched in her face, it confirmed everything. She turned her eyes to her captain and nodded. He gave her a nod of his own and turned to Tad's captain to make arrangements for the transfer of the case once again. Angela turned her attention back to Tad and motioned toward the door. He followed her inside. She led him up the stairs into the son's room.

"I check this room first. The son's death is always first and it's always the same." Angela stood at the doorway and allowed Tad to examine the room. His head followed the trail of blood spray from the bed to the wall. He pulled out gloves from his back pocket and pulled them on with a snap at the wrist before pulling back the son's covers on the bed. He crouched down next to the edge and leaned in close.

"Same type of stab wound at the carotid artery." He commented.

Angela noted to Tad how William pulled the blanket up over the son as if sleep. That stayed consistent. She motioned for Tad to follow her. He turned toward the daughter's room in the hallway but Angela called him back and advised that he wouldn't find the daughter there. Tad pursed his eyebrows in question.

"He made the father watch this time."

Tad's thumb scratched his eyebrow as his gaze fell to the floor.

"Do you need a moment?"

He shook his head, "no."

They continued down the hallway and back down the stairs to the dining room. Tad took in the scene before him. The father sat slumped in the chair facing toward a body lying on the floor. He walked over toward the father first.

He examined the wound on the stomach. It looked like the other crime scene photos he observed. He moved his attention to the mother. Unlike the father, her head fell back like she was looking up at the ceiling. He walked around her chair examining both arms, careful not to step on the blood puddle that soaked the sides of the chair.

"At least ten cuts here. All looking like different depths."

"Your M.E. will confirm."

"He'll be happy to see you, you know." His eyes darted up to meet hers and a small smile crept up his lips. "He's called me at least once a week to check on you."

"I'm sure he's calling to check on the case." She rolled her eyes.

"Oh no, he's taken a shine to you. He checks on the case too, but he's more interested in me making sure you're ok and you're not shouldering all of this alone. That I'm carrying my fair share."

She rolled her eyes again and told him to focus on what's in front of him. She leaned on the doorframe and watched him shift his focus to the daughter lying on display in front of her father. The bag still over her face. His head tilted at the blood coming out from under her back and leg.

"He stabbed her before suffocating her. Why? To incapacitate her?" He looked over at Angela but his eyes darted to the carpet between them. "Why are there spots of blood between you and me?"

Angela looked down and saw the droplets leaving a trail to the body. They followed the trail of blood drops to the front door. They went outside and asked the CSU team if they caught the drops of blood and if they swabbed the door for DNA and blood. The CSU team advised that they caught the droplets but had not swabbed the door at this time. Tad's captain ordered one man from the CSU team to swab the door while Angela and Tad continued their examination. Both captains joined the detectives in the home for their examination, careful to stand back and just observe. Tad and Angela went back to Sophie's body. Tad's gloved hand pointed to the cut places in her jeans.

"It looks like he stabbed her in the leg more than once. Why? He already stabbed her in the back. Why stab her in the leg multiple times?"

"Unless he stabbed her in the leg first and then stabbed her in the back." Angela responded.

"Then he suffocated her. Why the overkill?"

"The last time there was this much overkill, overheads tried to have me taken off the case. But, I don't think that's what happened here. Especially with the blood trail from the door. We'll get the lab results back to make sure, but I'd be willing to bet that it's Sophie's blood."

"I think that's a safe assumption since the trail leads to Sophie's body." Tad quipped.

"Don't be a smartass." She glared at him. "My point was that she pissed him off when she tried to make a getaway." She pointed over to the chair at the far side of the table. "See how that chair is pulled away from the table and it's kind of facing toward us? My guess is that he tied up Sophie and she got free. See how those arms on the chair are looking weird like they're not connected to that piece that's supposed to hold them up? She slipped out that way and she made a run for it. This was her punishment."

"You were in here a total of five minutes before you came and got me. You got all of that in five minutes?"

"CSU was taking pictures of the chair when I came into the dining room after checking the son's room."

He bobbed his head in understanding. "That makes more sense." He winked at her.

Angela thought to herself how he brought a sense of light to all this darkness before her. A darkness that pushed down against her shoulders, almost crushing her. He took on some of this burden. He joked and quipped because he knew how deeply she felt each and every wound inflicted on this family. She reminded herself that he probably also felt these wounds just as deeply and she was sure how his partner and family were torn apart in the same way sat firmly in the forefront of his mind right now.

"I can read your face, Partner. Let's just focus on the family in front of us. They deserve that respect."

"Says the man making jokes." She lifted her eyebrow at him.

"Oh, Tad's known for his jokes at crime scenes." Tad's captain interjected. "He likes to remind us that we all have to have some sort of morbid sense of humor in order to see what we see every day. And honestly as long as he's being respectful it's all taken in stride. Plus, even with the dumb humor, he never seems to miss anything at the scene."

"You have Nick to thank for that. Taught me everything I know."

"He'd say differently. He always said you had good instincts and a keen eye for details."

Tad just shrugged at that and continued his observations with Sophie's body.

"I'm going to have the rest of CSU come back in now if that's ok with you," asked Tad's captain to Angela.

She nodded yes, and the captain whistled at the CSU team to come back inside.

"You're missing the key detail, Tad." Angela said walking over to the table.

Tad stood up and followed her to where she stood.

"What am I—" His sentence trailed off as he read the message left in the father's blood.

The word DISTRACTION followed by the signature A sat on the plate as if he served the message for dinner. The captains walked over to read it as well.

"I think it's pretty clear this message was intended for you this time, Tad." Angela's captain stated as he peered over Tad's shoulder.

"Maybe, but whether or not I continue working this case, I'm already in his sights. He's not just going to forget me, even if I walk away right now."

Both captains voiced their agreement. The sickly look washed over Angela's face once again. Tad wanted to reach out his hand to comfort her, but he held strong. He'd have plenty of time later when she stayed at his house since the newest attack occurred in his hometown. He assumed they would stay at his place until they tied up loose ends and then they would continue as they had been working at her office and place. Once they finished their walk through and examination, Angela stopped Tad away from everyone else.

"Would you please catch a ride to your station with your captain? You can complete your paperwork and make sure we got all the evidence while you're there. I'm going to head back to my house. I can do my paperwork from my own office today and then come back to yours tomorrow. I'll request the 911 call as well. The same woman who forwarded me the last call should be able to locate and send me his call without issue. Cap needs to meet with your captain again tomorrow, so he'll bring your car to the precinct since he's already gotten permission to drive your vehicle to your station."

He thought about arguing, but her plan made the most sense, despite the fact that he believed it was just a convenient cover-up as to the real reason she wanted to go home alone. She's trying to push him back to arm's length.

To hell with that. He didn't open his mouth. He just nodded his head.

"Lane's already been notified that this is top priority, so he's cleared his schedule for the day. We should have the results of the autopsies later today. Obviously, we won't have the written report like last time or all the toxicology tests, but he should be able to go over cause of death and what he saw in his exam like last time. I'll get with him and tell him we'll come by first thing tomorrow morning." Tad said and Angela just nodded in reply.

"Hey," his voice lowered. Even though no one else was around, he still knew that he needed to keep his voice down just in case. "Look at me." Her sky-colored eyes met his, but she wasn't seeing him. He sighed. "Drive safe okay? Text me when you get to your house." She nodded.

As soon as she drove away, he spoke Captain Armstrong and requested he not drive his car from Angela's house to the station in the morning. Once he finished up his day here at his station, Tad would Uber to Angela's house. He told the captain that he would be damned if she was going to try and cut him out like she intended to when he first started working with her. They'd come too far, and he wasn't going to fall back just because this son of a bitch was pissed he was involved. The captain advised him that there was no need for Uber. He would stay at Tad's station until he was ready to go. He was going to Angela's house later that night anyway to convene over the new crime scene. It was a ritual of theirs. Tad thanked the man and told him that he would see him back at the station. Tad got into the car with the first responding officer and asked him about the 911 call and his first impressions on the scene.

— — —

Angela reached her house and walked into the front door. Gizmo met her at the door rubbing his body against her leg, demanding attention. She leaned down and scratched his ears. She noticed Gizmo looking at the door expectedly.

"He's not coming, Gizzie. Probably never again."

Gizmo looked up at her and meowed in protest. He allowed her once last scratch before running off to watch the road from the bay window in her front room. Angela grabbed her laptop bag from next to the door and walked down to the basement. She turned on the lights and the photos of the families greeted her with their ghostly, unavenged smiles. She set the bag on the desk and pulled out her laptop. She sat in her chair and turned on the computer. While she waited for the ever slow government computer to boot up, she turned to the murder board and wrote the Jones family's name in the free space. Seven families. Will this ever end? Will she ever catch up to him or will he always be one step ahead with a knife in his hand until he's ready to finally have the showdown they both knew was coming?

Once the computer booted up, she retrieved the number for her dispatch contact in Tad's city and called her. Becky agreed to send her the dispatch call within the hour. Angela pulled up her necessary reports and began typing what she saw. She silently thanked her captain that he didn't force her to make the death notifications for next of kin. By family number three, anyone who watched the news knew her name and connection to the case. After family number four and Jacquelyn's sister physically assaulting her, the captain determined that the local uniforms who initially responded to the 911 calls for each county should notify the families. Angela never pressed charges on Jacquelyn's sister because she understood her pain and anger. How could Angela not catch him? William wanted to be found. These families were his twisted version of hide and seek.

After doubling back to Tad's town, she wondered not for the first time when he would return to hers. Would her town be his grand finale? When would this finally end? When would he grow tired of butchering these families and face who he truly wanted to kill? She just needed him to make one mistake. One. Then she would have him. They would have the face off they both wanted. She stared at her father's journal next to her laptop and ran her thumb along the corner, making the paper flip. The spine frayed from how often she'd read her biological father's words. They didn't make her cry anymore and she just about knew them by heart. Mostly, she just ran her finger along the ink and traced the only thing she had left of him: his penmanship. Her mother never kept a single picture or anything of her biological father's belongings, not that Angela blamed her. Angela turned her attention to her dad's photo on the desk. Her heart ached with how much she missed him.

"I wish you were here to help me out. You always knew how to look at the problem from another angle to find the answer." *Just like Tad.*

Once she finished typing up her report, she checked her email. The 911 call sat waiting for her at the top of her inbox.

She forwarded it to Tad and her captain before opening up the file. She wrote the time of the call on the white board. Hopefully, Lane would be able to give a time of death close enough to determine if he made the call before or after the murder. She hit play. Her brother's voice filled her ears. He sounded the same in each call. Polite. A little out of breath. Excited. Always excited like all of this was great fun. She replayed it again. She closed her eyes to better hear any background noise. Just like the other calls, she couldn't hear anything notable in the background. She rubbed her eyes with the palms of her hands. She wrote down the number that called 911 and emailed it to a tech in her department to see if the phone could be located. He's never taken the time to turn them off because he used burners and he never worried about leaving them near the crime scene since he wasn't actually trying to hide his crime. She thought to herself how he had rushed this one, so maybe he had made a mistake this time. One could hope. Tomorrow after they met with Lane, they would go back to the crime scene and examine it further. Then came interviewing neighbors to see if they saw anything. Maybe Tad knew the area and could assist with locating security cameras. Her phone vibrated on her desk. She unlocked her phone and read the text from the captain saying that he got caught up at the station, but would be on his way later, right around dinner time. He wondered if she wanted their usual food, so she sent him a text back saying that was fine and he better not forget the soy sauce this time—please and thank you.

———

Later that evening, she heard footsteps coming down into the basement.

"Hey, how did everything go at the station with the other captain? Does he want to pull—" she turned around and saw Tad coming down the rest of the steps. "What are you doing here?"

He put the food down at the desk. "Cap is on the phone with his wife outside. First of all, I made sure you got your soy sauce, don't worry. Secondly, no, my captain doesn't want to pull me. He's pissed this mother fucker felt the need to circle back around to our town again, especially after killing one of our own last time. He knows we're going to get him. Third and finally," he pulled her into his arms and kissed her. "I know you wanted space, and how all of this just solidified how you felt before—about me not being on this case with you because it was unsafe. But you're just going to have to get over yourself honey, because we've already gone over this. I don't care if I have to sleep on the couch or in my cop car outside, you're not shaking me. The couch or my car is as much space as you're getting. Do you understand me? We're cops. Criminals getting pissed off at us all the time and us being in danger is in the job description."

She cupped his cheek and caressed his face with her thumb. He leaned forward and kissed her nose before winking at her. She rolled her eyes while a smile pulled at the corners of her lips.

"You're ridiculous," she said.

He turned his attention to the murder board. He walked over to the most recent family's name and pulled a picture from his back pocket. The Jones family's faces smiled at them. The sounds of Robert's footsteps thumped in their ears.

"Sorry, I was on the phone and then I went and got us forks. Oh good, it looks like y'all waited for me." He handed Angela a fork and then pulled out their food from the bag. Angela looked over at Tad who pulled out a burger from his white paper bag. He looked back at her.

"What? I didn't want Chinese. Days like this needs comfort food."

"That's so Lane of you," she joked.

The captain looked puzzled at the joke. She filled him in while they ate. Once they finished eating, they turned their attention back to William and the families.

"The family has already been notified. Uniforms did it not long after we left the crime scene. Mr. Jones' father and Mrs. Jones' sister. Both absolutely distraught. But, both agreed to meet with us within the next few days. The father wants more information about what happened to his son and family," said Tad.

"I think it's better that you talk with the father while I re-examine the crime scene," Angela answered.

"The father specifically requested to talk to both of us. He's devastated but he's not angry toward you. You need to talk to him to find out about the family." The captain slid the order into his words.

"Isn't that the benefit of having a partner?" Angela countered.

"Yes, but the father wants to talk to you too," said Tad.

She sighed. "Alright. Though, these interviews tend not to bring anything to the table." She examined the murder board. "William doesn't care about these families. I don't know how he picks them, but they are there because they meet his criteria. I wouldn't be surprised if he didn't remember their names."

19

"So, what do we bring to the ME's office today? More pie?" Angela asked through her car's speakerphone system.

Tad's laughter surrounded her. A warmth spread through her chest hearing the baritone. "It'll be eight in the morning by the time we get there. We're not going to be able to buy a burger or his wife's pie this early."

"What did you send him to eat yesterday?"

"His favorite BBQ. I even snuck him a soda. His wife doesn't like him drinking that stuff."

"She feeds him pie. What's the difference?"

"Hers is sugar filled with love. Soda is sugar filled with nonsense according to her."

Angela chuckled. "Can't argue with that logic I guess."

They talked the rest of the way to Tad's town. They speculated what else they'd find at the scene and why William stabbed Sophie then put a bag over her head. Angela gently reminded Tad that it wasn't about quick and painless with the daughters. Angela didn't need to see his face to know his goddaughter's death flashed across his mind. When they reached the ME's office, Lane greeted them at the door. His left hand held coffee while his right held the keys.

"Y'all are just in time. I finally finished everything late last night so forgive my gigantic coffee." Once he opened the door, he smiled at Angela. "I'd say it is nice to see you, but I'll say that next time when hopefully there isn't another dead family in my town."

She smiled and nodded at him. "I'll hold you to that."

Tad and Angela followed Lane down the hallway and into the autopsy room. Lane put down his coffee long enough to put his lab coat back on and put his keys into his lab coat pocket. He picked up the coffee and took a long pull before picking his file next to the bodies before them. He opened the file and browsed the contents one more time.

"Ok, so who do you want to start with?"

Angela and Tad simultaneously answered Lane. Tad said daughter while Angela advised him to start with the father. Lane looked between the two.

"Y'all might want to get on the same page."

"Father," Angela answered. "Y'all are aware that if this is William, three of the four family members' deaths don't change. I don't want to waste time if there is a variation proving this isn't William."

"I think we've already established this is the same guy, Detective. He wrote a note specifically for the both of us in blood." Tad retorted, irritation coating his words.

Lane cut in before Angela could open her mouth and tell Tad where he could stick his attitude.

"Now, I wouldn't want to presume to know more about this man than you do detective, and I know I've only ever done one other autopsy from this man's heinous crimes. But I would venture to say that it's the same man. I do want to bring something to your attention though."

Continue was all Angela said in response.

"He took a large knife to the father's stomach and disemboweled him. There are knife wounds on the intestines where he stabbed the father repeatedly. He slashed the mother's arms continuously until she bled out. That knife though was much smaller."

"Two different knives?" Tad asked.

"Precisely. Though, you have to remember detective that a larger knife would be beneficial for the father's murder due to the nature of disembowelment. He wouldn't need such a knife for the mother since hers were just overlapping cuts causing exsanguination."

"That's never stopped him before," spoke Angela.

"It's my understanding that y'all have one of the murder weapons, correct? He left it at the crime scene."

"Which is a twist all its own as well," Angela said.

"Yes, we have a knife from the crime scene. He left it next to Sophie's body," replied Tad.

"Large or small knife?"

Tad held up his hands and demonstrated the guesstimated length with his two pointer fingers.

"So, the smaller, pocket knife."

"Why would he keep one knife and leave the other?" Tad questioned.

"Lane, when you completed the autopsy on Nick and his family, the knife wounds were consistent with the large knife not the small knife from this crime scene, correct?"

Lane walked to the computer and pulled up Nick and his family's autopsies. He scrolled through his reports. "Large knife. Non-serrated. Most likely a hunting knife of some sort."

"That's what I thought. He used a large knife with the other families as well. That must be his knife that he uses at every crime."

"So, why use two different knives this time?" Lane asked.

"He left it by Sophie. Could it be Sophie's knife? Maybe it's the brother's?" Tad answered.

Angela turned to him. She rubbed her thumb across her bottom lip absently. "We've often speculated that he does recon on the home before the night of the attacks. We figure that's how he gets into these homes without being seen. We assume he scouts the neighborhood and watches the families in order to learn their routines. How else could he ensure that all the family members were home since he attacks at different times of the night? He's never given us any sort of definitive proof before. If this is Sophie's knife or even the brother's knife, it shows that he not only does recon within the neighborhood, but that he does recon inside the home."

"That's a bit of a stretch," commented Tad. "Couldn't he have just picked up the knife while he was there as a weapon of opportunity?"

"No, he's too methodical I think. Everything is completed a certain way. I don't think he would pick up a random pocketknife while he's there when he already had his own knife ready to go."

"Angela may have a point, Tad. He killed everyone in the family with this smaller knife except the father. Moving on to the brother. One quick, seamless stab into the jugular with that smaller knife. So, either the blade is the brother's blade and he just happened to come across it before he killed the boy or he had it ready to go."

"We'll dig around in the kids' rooms to see if we can figure out who the knife belongs to." Angela turned to Tad. "Will you call your forensics person and ask them to let us know what fingerprints come up with the knife?"

"Bobby is just going to tell me that he was going to do that anyway, but I'll call him now just to ask him if he's already dusted the knife for prints. You guys go on. Just don't get to the daughter without me." Tad muttered as he stepped out of the autopsy room to make the phone call in the hallway.

"Well, since we only have the daughter left, we can just chat while he waits." Lane looked at her with a smile and gave a fatherly wink.

Angela gave a faint smile back. She turned her attention to the bodies in front of them. Lane watched her eyes draw every inch of their faces into memory. She cut her eyes to Lane and gave a faint smile again. "So, no changes to the MO aside from using two different knives. This really is William, and William really did speed up his timeline with this family. We normally have a four-month pattern in between before he hits another family. Thank you for getting these autopsies completed for us, and thank you for verifying that this indeed is our case."

"Thank you for not counting Tad out and letting him on this case despite his personal attachments to it." Lane hesitated for a moment. "And to you."

She didn't look at him. Her eyes focused on the ground between the tiles on the floor, but he noticed the slight blush appearing on her cheeks.

"You should have been a detective, Lane. Your soft nature disarms people and you have a way of getting answers without asking any questions."

"Oh Detective, I already am one." Lane chuckled. "I just prefer to utilize my detective skills this way. Less backtalk."

She looked up to meet his gaze and he gave another good-natured wink at his own joke.

She chuckled back at him. "Fair enough I suppose."

Tad walked back into the room. "Bobby said he's working on dusting all the fingerprints. He hasn't done the knife yet, but he'll get to it soon. I told him to call once he had the fingerprints identified. He said it should be within the hour."

"He couldn't just dust the knife next?"

Lane and Tad shared a look.

"Well, it's a good thing you weren't on the phone with Bobby. He wouldn't take kindly to that remark." Lane commented.

"Bobby is meticulous. He's got a process and you can't mess with his process. If you mess with his process, he can't function. We'll have the results soon so no need to upset the man."

Angela cocked her eyebrow, but instead of responding turned her attention back to Sophie's body in front of them. "Lane, can you please go over what happened to the daughter?"

Lane's eyes went to Sophie's face. "This perp really doesn't like daughters." He paused a moment before continuing. "Victim, age fourteen, died of asphyxiation via the plastic bag over her face. But he did a number on her beforehand. He broke her nose. She has spots on the back of her head where hair was ripped out which suggests that he grabbed her by the hair at some point, and I would be willing to bet he drug her by the hair based on the amount removed. He stabbed her spine on the lower portion of her back." Lane indicated the place using Angela's back as the example. "Thus causing her to become immobile but not killing her. He wanted to make sure she didn't run again. Let's not forget the stab wounds to the upper right leg. Five in total."

"What makes you think that she ran?" Tad asked.

"Broken nose, pulled hair, stabbed to ensure that she was immobile...her hands were bound, but he wanted to make sure that her legs didn't work."

Tad smiled. "We found evidence at the scene to suggest that she ran before he killed her, but I wanted to see how you came to that conclusion. Damn, Lane. You should have been a detective."

"I'll tell you what I just told Miss Angela over here while you were on the phone. I already am a detective. I just utilize my skills differently than y'all do."

Angela smiled at Lane. "Thank you, Lane. I hope next time I see you it will be under different circumstances."

He returned the smile. "Me too. You and Tad will find this monster and stop him then we'll do a barbecue to celebrate. Just like Tad and Nick used to do at the end of a big case."

Angela looked at Tad using her peripheral vision. A sad smile crossed his face. She wanted to put her arms around him and comfort him, but they had both agreed that during work hours they weren't anything more than partners. It wasn't fair to Nick and his family or the other victims if their focus wasn't completely on William while on the clock. Angela watched Tad nod at Lane and tell him that he would continue to keep him updated off the record. They turned and left the building, getting into their cars and heading toward the Jones' family home.

———

Angela and Tad reached the Jones' home twenty minutes later. They walked under the yellow police tape and Tad signed in with the officer posted at the scene before they went inside the home.

"Do you want to split up, or do you want to examine the scene together?" asked Angela.

"I think we should examine the rooms together since you're the expert. I don't want you to have to go over a room I've examined because you're afraid that I've missed something. I was the expert at the last scene since it was my family. This is different."

"Plus, I'll be looking a little differently since he's changed up his timeline. I am hoping I'll find a mistake he wouldn't normally make."

"You don't normally look for a mistake on his part?" Tad teased.

She glared at him before she turned toward the steps and walked up to the second floor.

"We'll start in the son's room since it might be his knife," she called down to him. She heard the thump of his footsteps as he ran up the stairs to catch up to her. They made their way to the son's room and opened the door. The coroners left the sheets pulled down to reveal the blood stains left behind. Angela and Tad agreed to take opposite sides of the room to go over anything that may look out of place.

"You know, for a teenage boy this kid sure kept his room neat as a pin," Angela commented.

"I would bet you anything his mother kept it looking like this. I know my mom would get onto me constantly about my room being dirty and then getting so fed up that she just cleaned the damn thing herself every so often. I always caught hell for it later, but at least I didn't have to do it."

Angela examined the window. She noticed the alarm and opened the window to test if it worked. When it didn't make a chirp or a beep, she inspected the device and found the wire cut but just close enough to where it wouldn't be noticed at first glance. Tad's face leaned in beside hers.

"Do you think he cut it?" Tad asked.

Angela looked down at the roof. Tucked in beside the window sat a box of cigarettes. She leaned out and picked them up. "My money is on the son since I'm sure his parents didn't approve of their teenage son smoking. And my money is also on him keeping his room this clean so his mom wouldn't find his contraband while she was cleaning up in here."

Tad shook his head. "All teenagers have secrets."

"Oh yeah? What was yours?"

He smiled. "Condoms. My mom was a good Southern Baptist woman who would have beaten me for having premarital sex."

She laughed. "Ah yes, I remember you telling me about her now."

"What about you?" Tad asked, as he went back to examining his side of the room.

"I didn't really have anything hidden in my room. Not really. My mother got me on birth control as soon as I hit puberty because she didn't want any sort of scandal. Ironic really, considering who my biological father is and the fact that they got married because she was pregnant. I knew better than to keep cigarettes and alcohol in my room considering my dad was a cop. I always made sure that I was out of the house if I was going to partake in anything illegal. I thought in my teenage brain that I could pull a fast one on my parents when I lied about where I was going or what I was doing. It wasn't until years later when I was an adult that my dad informed me that he knew what I was up to but he knew that he raised me right and had to let some things slide because rebellion was a part of being a teenager."

"The more you tell me about your dad, the more I know I would have liked the man."

Angela looked over at Tad and smiled. "I think he would have liked you too."

Tad finished going through the last drawer in the desk and shut it. "You know, besides the cigarettes that you found, I don't see anything in this room that says to me that the knife was his. I haven't seen any other knives and normally if you have one, you have more. At least for boys."

"Girls, too. I had quite the collection of knives when I was a teenager. My mother always used to purse her lips and shake her head whenever she saw me with one."

Tad's phone rang against his hip. He saw Bobby's name across the screen and clicked the accept button on the touchscreen. "Hey Bobby, what you got for me?" He listened for a moment and thanked Bobby before hanging up. "Turns out there is only one set of prints on the knife."

"Let me guess... Sophie's?"

"Ding ding ding! We have a winner! Sponsors, tell her what she's won!" Tad motioned over to the window and paused as if listening to a reply. "You, Angela Burns, have won a trip down to the daughter's room to examine any evidence left behind!"

Angela rolled her eyes. "Ok, so now we know that the knife didn't belong to the son. Neither one of us has found anything pertaining to the investigation in here. Let's move over to Sophie's room."

They left the room and made their way to Sophie's room at the end of the hallway. They opened the door and Tad once again commented about the room's tidiness. Angela bet she could wipe her finger on any surface before the crime techs got to this room and not come back with any dust. Once again, Angela took one side while Tad took the other. They searched all the drawers and the closet. Everything sat in the spaces with perfect organization, nothing out of place.

"Secrets," whispered Tad. He checked the alarm on the window. He noted that it was sliced just like the other one. He looked under the window for a pack of cigarettes like the brother. He tilted his head. Ashes... but no pack like the brother. He wondered where she hid hers if not under the window.

"She smoked too," Tad said to Angela. "But there are no cigarettes here. Maybe she shares with her brother?"

"Would a brother share his contraband with his sister like that?"

"Probably not," Tad answered, as he sat down at the daughter's desk. The ceiling fan light reflected off the wood flooring. He squinted his eyes. "Why are there scuff marks like the bed was moved?"

"It's a wood floor. I'm sure the bed moved sometimes. I know mine does and I have to move it back." Angela responded without looking at him, preoccupied as she opened the drawers for the second time, hoping to see something she missed.

"Are there scuff marks at the top of the bed too?"

She looked at him. Her eyebrow raised in annoyance.

"Just humor me, ok?"

She sighed and pulled a flashlight out of her pocket. She shined it toward the headboard. "I don't see anything."

"That's what I thought," he said kneeling onto the floor and moving the bottom portion of the bed to trace the scuff marks on the floor. "I've never seen this outside of movies, but I can't help but wonder..."

"Wonder what?" Angela sat and watched Tad knock on the flooring. "What the hell are you—"

"HA!" Tad called. "He pulled out his key ring and pushed one of his keys against the seam. "It's too big. I wish I had a—" Angela slid a closed knife across the floor. He picked it up with a look of confusion on his face.

"I warned you." She shrugged.

"We've been working together this long and I never knew you were packing a knife?" He held up his hand and shook his head. "Never mind. I forget you think you're a woman of mystery and all that."

He pried up the piece of flooring and closed the knife before sliding it back over to her. "Let's see what we have here." Tad pulled out the contents of the hiding place with his gloved hands. "Smokes...a journal..." He dug his arm in further. "Pictures...I think that's it... No, wait. There is something else tucked into this corner here. Oh, look at that, another knife!"

Angela smiled. "So, I think it's safe to assume that the parents didn't know about the knife, and that William does recon beforehand. I mean, what are the chances he comes across this hiding space during the murder?"

Tad tilted his head and squinted his eyes, thinking hard. "You know his habits better than I do. But you've always called him meticulous, and said that he has a certain way of doing things. William comes in and out of the home undetected. He doesn't ever break, and he's bypassed multiple alarm systems. No neighbors ever hear screams and there are never 911 calls made from the home until he calls in the murders. All of these point to recon."

"Now we know he doesn't just do recon the outside of the home. He goes inside."

"But why take the knife?" Tad questioned.

She shrugged. "Now that I can't answer. Let's bag up the rest of this stuff and have your lab guys see if they can get anything off any of this."

"We should also check with the neighbors to see if any of them have security cameras that would pick up anything toward the road or pointing at the Jones' home. We can also check if there are any traffic cams or security cameras at local businesses that might have caught him doing his recon. Maybe we can catch his face on a camera and get a more updated picture to show the public."

Angela agreed. They bagged up the evidence and headed out of the home. They knocked on the neighbor's doors around the cul-de-sac and left their business cards wedged in the door jams when no one answered. They stopped by the local shops and obtained all their security footage. They decided to grab lunch at the local diner before going through the security footage. Unfortunately, the shops only had footage from the past forty-eight to seventy-two hours, if any footage at all. Angela and Tad hoped they could find something on those tapes. While they waited for their food, Mrs. Anderson from next door called them back. She said that she didn't have any sort of security system with a camera. She joked that she was too old for that "new-fangled technology." She can barely work the system her adult children convinced her to invest in, where she has to do is insert a passcode to arm and disarm the system. She commented on how it came in handy a few days ago, proving no one broke into her house even though the police came to the door stating they had received a 911 about a break-in at her residence. They were able to confirm with the alarm company that everything was as it should be, and it was just a false alarm. Angela agreed with her that it was a good thing, and thanked her for her time before hanging up the phone. She and Tad went back to his station and sat their stuff down in the conference room. Angela pulled out her laptop and inserted the USB drive with the footage from the local shops.

"Back where it started," Tad commented, sitting down in the same seat he'd sat in when they first met.

She looked at him while the computer booted up. "Let's just hope that we have better luck than we've had so far."

Tad's phone rang. He quickly swallowed the bite of burger he took before accepting the call. He spoke to the neighbor for a minute or two before thanking the man, and stated that they would be back by within the hour. The neighbor on the line spoke, and Tad gave him his email address. He thanked him again and hung up.

"What was that all about?"

"The neighbor across the street called back stating that they actually did have one of those doorbells with a camera. He said that it's normally triggered by them coming home and that nothing else can really be seen on the recordings. They're all only about ten seconds long anyway. I told him that we could come by and get the recordings from him, but he just said that he'd email them to me. He thinks it's a waste of our time, but he wants to do anything he can to help us. He said that the Jones' son used to walk their dog before it died, and that they were good folks. He said I should be getting them within an hour or so."

"Good, maybe we'll get lucky and find something."

20

Alexander sat on the white comforter atop of his all white sheets, courtesy of every halfway hotel he's ever used. His leather-bound journal lay flat to his left with his pen enveloped neatly in the middle seam. The TV was turned on to the local news station, but his mind wasn't focused on whatever fluff piece the local anchorman man was discussing with the anchorwoman sitting next to him. Alexander was sure that the anchorwoman was only hired because she was beautiful and blonde, not because she had any actual talent. Her only contribution to the conversation was agreement with the anchorman and a smile that looked good on camera. No, his mind turned instead to recent events. He rubbed his lip, remembering the bag sucking in and out of Sophie's mouth as she tried desperately to breathe in any air that thinned with each inhale.

Captain Armstrong's voice filled Alexander's ears, pulling him back to the present. The captain stood with his shoulders back and held high like a man in charge. Alexander chuckled. The reporters were going to tear him apart. Family number seven in two years... doesn't look good for dear ole' captain. And he was sure that they were no closer to catching him. His eyes turned to his sister's face, standing to the captain's left just a little way behind him. Her face was stoic, but her eyes continued to look down and away from the cameras. At least she felt a little shame for being such a terrible player. He didn't have any other siblings either to play with growing up, but he still turned out to be great at hide and seek. Alexander's eyes darted to the figure standing next to Angela. He bared his teeth. *Tad. What did I say about Tad? Hadn't I made myself clear?*

"The two detectives standing behind me are tirelessly working on this case and have made progress. However, I cannot discuss an ongoing investigation. That being said, I will not be answering any questions at this time." Captain Armstrong turned around and headed back inside the station.

"Detectives, huh?" Alexander spat. "Detectives." His hands trembled and he felt heat rise to his cheeks. He closed his eyes and tilted his head side to side to loosen himself.

"My phone call and my words written in the last father's blood wasn't enough for you?" He snarled. He paced around the room. He pulled his knife from his pocket and flicked it open and closed with each step he took. He pictured walking up to the receptionist who had flirted with him and gutting her right there in the lobby. He pushed the tip of the knife into his right palm to center himself. He closed his eyes and blew out a breath.

"Can't kill whomever I want like that again until after the game is over," he reminded himself. "The receptionist can be the first once this is all over."

He took off his clothes and folded them onto the chair next to the bed. He put the journal on the little dinette table. He pulled his running clothes out of his gym bag and put them on. After he laced up his shoes, he grabbed his keys. He would stretch at the park. Or maybe he wouldn't stretch. A little pain while running might help him focus.

He reached the local park and slid the car into the front row facing the central playground. He stared at the children swinging on swings and sliding down slides. He watched kids chase each other around playing tag. A little boy no older than nine chased a screaming bunch of girls around the park in attempts to make whoever he could catch "it." Alexander understood that game. It's a crude, juvenile version of his own. Sometimes you have to chase after the easiest target instead of the one you really want, the one that taunts and teases you about how much better they are than you, and that's why you can't get them. *I could slaughter each and every one of these families and they'd never think it was me.* He smiled to himself. He got out of the car and walked to the start of the running trail that ran through the woods surrounding the park. He liked that it encompassed each facet of the park. It covered the soccer fields, the football field, the baseball field, and the little playground where he started most of his runs. He could wander each parking lot without worry of suspicion, because each field had its own entrance to the running trail, and all he had to do was hold out his keys. No one looked suspicious if they were just looking for their car after a good run. He reached the front of the trail and put on his running mix. The melody of a violin flooded his ears as he began his run. He felt his feet hit the trail with each step. The trees fell behind him as he picked up his pace. His breath found a rhythm in the strides. His mind floated away from the people passing him in opposite direction. His thoughts turned to Angela. His vision blurred and he felt all the blood rushing to his ears. He heard each beat of his heart pounding over the violin that was supposed to calm him. *How dare she?* How dare she do this knowing this was supposed to be between the two of them? He pictured Tad. He sees his hands soaked in Tad's blood as he shoved the knife into his chest over and over. The cough of blood in his mouth and on his face as he screams. They all scream, no matter how much of a man they think they are. He wonders how much force it would take to crack open the ribs so he could mail Angela his heart. His feet stop and a smile crosses his face. The woman walking her dog notices, and she gives him a smile in return. Laughter crawls out of Alexander's mouth at the idea. He leans forward with his hands on his knees as his laughter fills the space. The woman's smile falters and she keeps her peripheral gaze upon him, like prey who tries to go unnoticed past the occupied predator. She speeds up her steps into a near jog. Alexander finishes his laughing and then continues down on the trail. He'll finish his run now that he has a plan.

— — —

He opened the door to his hotel room. His clothing and hair stuck to his body with the Georgia humidity. He stripped off his clothing and turned on the shower. He stepped under the frigid water and felt the sting cool his body temperature. After washing off, he dressed in jeans and a white t-shirt. He didn't need to stand out when he put the journal in the mailbox. He crouched down to the black suitcase in the closet. He unzipped it and counted the stack of composition books. William Senior was consistent with his books. Each the same, those black and white composition books used in school. Alexander stacked them based on year, the earlier years on the bottom. Some years were missing, and Alexander had thrown away a couple of books from the later year, as they were too damaged to be read from what looked and smelled like alcohol spills. He pulled out the bottom book. Angela had the first book their father had started writing in once she was born. He thumbed through the pages until he found the entry he was looking for. He smiled to himself. He got up from the closet and sat down at the table. He opened to the last page of his journal and tore it out. He grabbed his pen and wrote a message before using it as a bookmark. If she didn't get the message this time, Tad's death was on her. His mind turned to the words she would read regarding what their father wanted to do to the imposter who had stolen his title. Alexander's smile grew wider. He'd been looking forward to using this method with a woman after he grew tired of this game and killed Angela. But killing Tad this way had its own appeal. He grabbed his keys and headed for Angela's house.

Once he reached her house, he stopped his car next to the mailbox and got out to place the notebook inside. He shifted his eyes, taking in his surroundings, but the neighborhood sat quiet during the day, waiting for everyone to come home from work. He went back into his car and drove to the nearest gas station. He pulled out his cell and dialed the station. When the office secretary answered, he politely asked for Detective Burns and waited to hear his sister pick up the line.

"Detective Burns," she spoke formally into the phone.

"You know, younger sisters are supposed to listen to their older brothers."

The line went silent a moment before she answered. "Considering we've never formally met, William, I guess I never learned how to act like a little sister."

He shut his eyes and smiled. *Baby sister has balls.*

"I don't go by William, as you well know. And you don't seem surprised to hear from me."

"I expected a phone call before now. So no, your voice is not unexpected. And if you don't go by William, what am I supposed to call you? 'A' doesn't really sound appropriate, despite how it's how you sign your notes to me."

"Still haven't figured out what A means? My my my, I gave you too much credit."

"My guess is you go by your middle name, but we've never spoken for me to confirm it with you," she retorted.

"Ah. Maybe I did give you enough credit after all." He chuckled. "Anyway, we don't have long. We both are so busy after all. I just wanted to call and remind you that if you continue to have this man involved in our game, his death will be on your hands."

He was met with silence.

He waited.

"Did you hear me?" he asked again through clenched teeth.

"I heard you," she responded.

Alexander pulled out his knife and sat opening and closing it against his leg.

"And yet you don't listen. I'm sure you wouldn't want Tad to die the way your stepfather should have died all those years ago. The way our father planned it."

"And what way is that, William?" She challenged him with his name.

"Check your mailbox and find out."

He hung up the phone and tossed it out of his window before leaving the gas station and heading back to the hotel. He might need another run.

21

Angela stood with the phone in her fist, only a slight tremble betraying her as she attempted to mask her face behind a wall of apathy. Her brother's voice echoed in her ear. She'd heard it in recordings but hearing him now—threatening Tad now—sent a chill down her spine. Tears pricked at her eyes but she bit her tongue to stop them from falling. She wouldn't let him affect her, especially not in the precinct and in front of Tad.

"I have to go home. Now." Her words came out strong despite how she felt.

Tad didn't have to ask who had been on the other side of that conversation. Even if he hadn't heard her side of the call, her change in demeanor would have given it away. He wanted to argue with her. He wanted to hold her. He wanted to send himself through the phone and put his hands on William himself. Instead he just nodded his head. Angela hung up the phone and gathered her belongings. Tad met her at the conference room door where they worked. They had shut the blinds when they walked in earlier. He put his arms around her waist. She didn't move under his touch. Her face turned to the door. He gently put his fingers under her chin and guided her face to meet his eyes. Her blue eyes met his and he leaned in to kiss her. She didn't pull away, but instead leaned in to meet his lips. Soft and slow.

"Honey—" he started to speak, but she just shook her head.

"You're right. I'll start up the car and wait for you to gather your stuff and give the heads up to your captain about us leaving and why."

He resisted a smile. She's finally accepted that he wasn't going anywhere. "Are you going to call Cap on the way to your house?"

"Yes. I'm sure he'll want to meet us there, but there isn't much point. He wouldn't have called to give me the heads up if it was a trap. Plus he threatened you, not me. He expects me to bend to his will with whatever this gift is. I suspect it's another of my biological father's journals."

"Ok. Go ahead and call him while you're waiting for me. I shouldn't be long. I am not even sure Cap is in his office. If he's not, I will leave him a note on his desk."

He watched her leave and head out the door. He quickly packed up his work stuff and headed to the captain's office. He rapped his knuckles against the closed door and waited for Archer's voice to tell him to come in. No reply came. He opened the door and went over to the desk. As always, the captain left his phone in his office, so it must be lunch time, and he normally went home to spend it with Evelyn. Ever since the captain's wife threatened to leave him last year, he always left his phone in the office and took a proper lunch because she appreciated him giving her his full attention, even if he could only give it to her during his lunch hour. Tad couldn't blame the man for leaving his phone at his desk. Evelyn was a good woman, and there are more important things than the job. Nick taught him that. Nick taught them all that. Tad grabbed a sticky note and a pen from the desk drawer and advised the captain where he was going, and that he wouldn't need backup at his place tonight. He advised he would call later with an update. He stuck it to the middle of the computer screen and then let himself out of the office before heading to the car.

"Ready?" Tad questioned as he buckled in his seatbelt.

She cut her eyes at him and put the car into drive.

"So, fill me in on the other half of your phone conversation while we drive."

She cut her eyes at him again. "I'm sure you got the gist of the conversation, and it wasn't very long as you witnessed."

"Still…this goes back to partners not having any secrets."

She sighed but began to tell him as they headed toward the house.

They reached the house and Angela parked the car next to the mailbox. She got out and went to the mailbox. She pulled out a composition notebook from inside. She handed it to him so she could pull the car into the garage. Tad examined the book. The pages were worn and yellowed with age. The spine was taped together with old duct tape, the only thing holding the contents together. About a third of the way through the book Tad noticed a piece of paper that didn't match the others coming out from the top of the book. The car stopped and they headed inside to the kitchen. He placed the book on the island and sat down while Angela made coffee.

"There seems to be a note in the pages," he said, breaking the silence.

Angela grabbed the book from the island and examined the top. She opened the book and pulled out the bookmark. Her eyes darted across the torn page as she read the words before her. She handed the note to him.

"At least it's not in blood this time," she quipped.

"And he didn't give you a note with the other journal, right?"

She shook her head.

Last warning. 3 strikes and he's dead.

"I would say that we should be wearing gloves because of fingerprints but—"

"There won't be any, and I don't plan on these ever seeing the light of day," she responded.

"What if there are others?" Tad questioned.

Her eyes met his and he didn't need her to respond to know the answer to his question. None of those journals were ever going to see the light of day either. Not if she and the Captain could help it.

Fair enough.

Tad nodded at the notebook splayed open. "So?"

She looked down at the entry in front of her and began

to read aloud:

December 11, 1993

They came to my job My fucking job! Couldn't find where I lived they
said... bullshit I say. They're fucking cops who came to my job instead of
where I live so they could make me sign away my rights. I told him to go
to Hell, but he told me I didn't have a choice. I can sign away my
rights now without a fuss or they would make me by taking me to
court and what judge is going to let me keep my rights when Kristen
has proof that I had delusions of killing my daughter? I guess I knew
this day was coming. Kristen won't even let me see her anyway. The
guy even offered me money. Told me it was worth it because he
loves his daughter so much... his daughter, not mine. I almost didn't
take it. He sat it down on the hood of my car as he walked
away knowing that I wasn't going to run him down and make him
take it back. His partner or whoever this guy was just stood there with
his nightstick in his hand. As if I would attack a pair of cops let
alone attack said cops at my job It's the only thing I have, and I
can't lose it. So, I signed the paperwork

I need a drink...

She stopped and squinted.

"This part is going to be more difficult to read. His
handwriting gets worse. I guess because he went and got
that drink, and a few more to go along with it. Bear with me
while I decipher it."

That fucking guy Jackson whatever his name is that fucking guy came to my job and forced me to sign away my daughter! He acted as if I would have actually ever hurt her! That's what the medication and the drinking and the therapy is for! But I could hurt him. Oh yes sir I could hurt him right good. I wouldn't make it fast either. Not like shooting him in the back of the head like one of those punk gang members. No. I would kill him slow. Enjoy it even. That's what Kristen deserves. She ruined my life. I'll get him on the job. Maybe tazer the partner since he threatened me with that nightstick. I'll tazer Jackson too. Just so I can get him to where he can't fight back. I'll even use his own handcuffs to make sure his hands stay behind his back. I imagine he'll look at me with those cop eyes and I will pluck them out. A knife should make that easy enough. My face will be the last thing he sees before he's writhing on the ground screaming. I won't let that last too long though. I'll take my knife and drag it across his throat so he can choke on his own blood. Then, I'll dump his body in front of Kristen's house. I'll ring the doorbell in hopes that she'll be the one to answer the door and I can hear her scream in terror at her dead husband on her doorstep.

Her eyes scanned the rest of the page. "No need to keep going. The rest looks like just a bunch of babbling."

"Well, that's quite a way for me to go…" Tad said, leaning back in his chair.

"That's not funny," she glared.

"Who was making a joke?" He retorted. He cleared his throat. "You said you didn't know your dad wasn't your biological father, right?"

"No, I didn't. They always told me that I was in the wedding pictures because they didn't want to get married right away after they found out about me. They didn't want people to think that he only wanted to get married because mother was pregnant. I guess that was a passive aggressive dig, since that's exactly what my mother did before. Later, when the truth came out, Mother told me that this was my dad's Christmas gift to her because she was always worried that my biological father would come back at some point and try to be in my life again. He gave her this peace of mind. It's actually kind of sweet if you think about it. Not the lying to me part of course, but that he did that for her and for me."

Tad studied her face as she recalled the memory. He watched a small smile tug at the corners of her mouth. "Every story you tell me about your dad just reinforces how much of a good man he was and how much you loved him."

She turned her attention to him. "He wasn't perfect. He was demanding and expected a lot from me. Mother would have told you that at times he worked too hard and was too tenacious in his pursuits. But yeah, my dad was a really good man. He loved and understood me even when Mother hounded me about being 'unlady-like.' He's the one who convinced Mother to let me go to the police academy without too much of a fuss. She never would have supported me going into this line of work if it weren't for him. She loved my dad and was proud that he was a detective, but she didn't want me to follow in his footsteps. My dad kept us connected. After he died, it pretty much just turned into obligatory Sunday dinners."

"Up until she passed away last year."

Angela nodded.

"Understood. Well, let's change gears here. We can put this journal with the other one downstairs and go back to focusing on the newest family and any footage we can gather to keep this moving."

"You're right. Let's bring our stuff downstairs and get back to work. I'll call Cap and let him know we're here, and that William just gave me another journal to review."

Gizmo leapt unto the island between them and meowed. Angela picked him up and kissed his head.

"Yes, buddy. You can come too."

———

Hours later they sat in front of their laptops with nothing left to watch. Angela's eyes burned as she rubbed them to try and get some relief. Tad twisted in his seat and Angela heard pops coming from his back before he sighed.

"You sounded like someone just broke a glow stick," she joked.

"That's what happens when you get old. You'll see. Thirty hits you like a rock. Nick used to tell me to wait until I was in my forties and then I would really know about everything popping when you sit too long. I really need to get up outta this chair and properly stretch my legs and body."

"I came at just the right time then, because food is upstairs." Captain Armstrong called as he came down the basement stairs. "I thought BBQ would be a nice change from burgers and fries."

Tad thanked him before running up the stairs toward the kitchen. Angela sat at the computer with her hands folded under her chin.

"What's up, Burns?"

Her gaze flicked up from the laptop to meet his brown eyes. She saw more and more crinkles around his eyes and deeper bags underneath them the longer this case continued. This case hadn't just aged her. "Nothing. We sat here for hours watching this stupid security camera doorbell thing and he managed to avoid it."

"The man did say that it only came on when triggered, so it's not like there was a high chance that he would happen to go by when it was triggered." He motioned for her. "Come on now. We'll discuss all this while we eat. I got your favorite."

She got up and followed him up the stairs. Tad already had a mouthful of BBQ sauce from his pulled pork sandwich dripping down his chin.

"You got a little something..." Angela motioned to his entire face, "right about here."

Tad licked around his mouth. Angela laughed as she handed him a napkin. Robert watched the interaction with interest. She didn't laugh like that often, not since her father died, and especially not with her chasing her killer brother all over Georgia. Tad had broken her barrier and she had reached an ease not many ever see. He knew Angela didn't plan on making it out alive. She'd finish the job, but she expected him to take her out with him. Robert clenched his jaw. He wasn't ok with that, and he had told her multiple times that he wouldn't see her dead. She always just replied with a shoulder shrug and told him that she would die if she had to. Real Sherlock Holmes and Moriarty type nonsense. But maybe, just maybe, Tad would give her the strength to fight harder to survive.

"So, do you want to wait until after you eat for us to run through everything?" Robert asked switching into captain mode as he grabbed his box of ribs.

"You mean for the millionth time?" Tad responded around his loaded cheeks.

"Might as well go through everything afterwards because I can't watch this man try and talk while chewing up BBQ," Angela laughed.

Tad put his finger to his nose in agreement before wiping his mouth again and audibly gulping. "My bad, honey. I didn't realize my eating habits offended your feminine sensibilities."

"I'll show you feminine sensibilities if you don't watch it, mister!" The smile curling up the edges of her mouth voided all the fire within Angela's glare.

The captain smiled again, watching their banter. "After the meal it is."

After dinner, they made their way back down to the basement. Captain asked Angela to run down everything from the beginning. Angela talked through the recent family's crime scene and what Lane had found during the family's autopsies. Angela reported that they finally had definitive evidence that William scopes out the family home before the night of the murders based on the knife that was used to kill every member of the family aside from the father, because his COD required a bigger knife. The captain advised that the evidence was weak but plausible. Angela reminded him that William is methodical, and Lane confirmed the brother was killed with the knife, yet fingerprints confirmed the knife belonged to the sister, due to her fingerprints being the only ones on the knife in question. If it belonged to the brother, or the brother had previously taken the knife from his sister, his fingerprints would likely be on the knife as well. Tad chimed in, stating that they also found another knife in the sister's secret hiding place under the floorboard of the bed. Captain held up his hands in surrender and relented that they made their case. Angela continued on anyway, stating that the killer also ensures that every member of the family is home and in bed, since the brother is always killed there. Lastly, the family never screams. He kills the brother before he has a chance to scream, and then uses the sister to subdue the parents. Once he kills them, he calls 911.

"Except for families two and five. He called before the murders," Angela continued.

Tad reviewed his notes about the 911 calls. "Wait... I know you've said before and after the murders before, but I don't think I paid attention to that since all the calls were worded the same way with exception of Brooklyn's family. And that was because he was trying to prove a point. Otherwise, he always states that a family was killed. Past tense, not future tense. Why? Why would he call in those murders before they actually occurred?"

"Unknown. We do know that those murders appear to be carried out more swiftly. Less time taken with the daughter to make her suffer."

"Of course, because they had to be. He only had a limited amount of time before the cops showed up. My question though, is how would he know just how much time he had to get in and get out unless he was just taking a chance?"

"No, he's too methodical for that." Angela thought for a moment and then slapped her hand on the table. "Of course!"

Tad looked at her. "Of course what?"

She pointed at Tad. "Of course you would ask that question! The most obvious question on the planet!"

He frowned at her. "I was just—"

"Asking the one question that we never thought to ask ourselves," she finished for him. She turned her attention to Captain Armstrong. "The kind of question dad would ask."

The captain smiled at her. "How would he know that he had enough time to kill those two families but not the others? Response time."

Angela smiled back. "Fucking response time."

22

Alexander sat at the picnic table next to the park. He rolled his neck around to stretch his tense muscles. He wasn't used to getting this restless already in the waiting period, but these last two families left him hungry for more sooner. It didn't help that he'd seen multiple families who fit what he was looking for. None of them seemed quite right though. It'd been one long month and even running left him unsoothed. He unscrewed the lid of his water bottle and tilted his head back to take a big gulp while his eyes remained on the siblings walking toward him. He could tell their relationship based on the body language. The brother held his keys in left hand while using the other to scold the glowering preteen. He caught a fraction of the conversation as they passed him. *Ask and you shall receive, as the old bitch used to say.* He scratched the corner of his open mouth to avoid anyone noticing his smile.

"Mom is going to have a cow! You know that right?"

Alexander wondered what the daughter did to cause such a reaction. He rose from the picnic table and began to walk in their same direction, careful to keep his headphones in his ears and changing the song on his phone occasionally to throw off suspicion from any cautious, watchful parent who might take notice that he got up not long after they passed him. He kept the volume almost on mute so he could listen to the conversation between the two siblings. He tended to pass unnoticed as far as he could tell; but parents—especially mothers—kept close eyes on single men around children. He followed them to the parking lot before swiveling his head and acting as if he couldn't remember where he had parked his car. His car sat two lanes across and fifteen cars down. He watched the siblings turn and each take a side around a green Toyota, likely a hand-me-down from their mother who upgraded. Alexander switched lanes so he didn't appear to be following them. He pulled out his phone to appear as if he was changing songs and pointed the camera lens toward the siblings, then snapped a photo. He smiled to himself and walked back to his car. Once he got inside, he zoomed in on the picture to confirm he got all the information he needed.

"Now comes the fun part," he whispered to himself. He put the car into gear and headed toward the hotel.

———

Alexander sat on his hotel bed with his laptop on his lap. His fingers raced across the keys as he accessed the DMV database. He pulled up the picture on his phone and typed in the license plate information into the designated space. A moment later the information popped up, revealing the owner of the car. Matthew Wallace. The father, based on the license information. Alexander copied the address and typed it into the box. The information for two more household members popped up underneath the father's information. Diane and

Peter Wallace. Alexander pulled up the son's information: seventeen years old. No daughter popped up, but he knew she existed. She just must not be old enough to drive, or the parents didn't want her to get her license yet even if she was old enough. Alexander doubted that was the case. The daughter looked barely pubescent. Alexander pulled up social media next. The parents shared a social media account filled with family memories and the father's real estate agent ads. The family consisted of the four of them: just his type. The children had accounts on all the platforms. Hadley Wallace had just turned fourteen. He wondered whether she'd be as feisty as Sophie based on the conversation he had overheard the two having in the park. He searched for any signs of a dog that would throw off his plan. He had managed to avoid any dogs with the previous families. He didn't mind killing a dog if needed. It's not like he hadn't before. His first kill had been a dog. A yippy little dachshund named Bowser. Or maybe it was Baxter. Whatever its name was, it belonged to the little neighbor girl named Cassidy. She wouldn't ever let Alexander play. She called him weird as she went by his house while walking that dog. She didn't call him weird or walk by his house ever again after she found her little dog dead in the backyard.

He pulled himself back to the present and reminded himself that he needed to focus. No dogs. They caused an unavoidable roadblock when he did his run-through. Alexander pulled up the parents' page once more and scrolled through the pictures. The father didn't post much, but two weeks prior he had posted a photo of a dog lying at his feet under the desk. Alexander clicked on the photo to read the caption. *My office buddy relaxing after a hard day of writing up offers*. He raked his hands down his face. Of course they had a dog. He knew he'd been itching too hard to find another family. He clicked on the comments below the photo. Beatrice Hendley asked if the office buddy went with him to work every day. Matthew responded that Max, because of course the dog's name was Max, came to work with him each day unless he had some sort of class. Alexander's frustration immediately melted.

"I can work with that," he smiled.

He looked at the father's ad on his page. Underneath his phone number sat his email address.

"Oh look at that... I bet his appointment calendar is attached to his email. That shouldn't be too hard to find out."

Within a few minutes he had the father's calendar laid out across his laptop screen. Appointments filled the calendar, but no classes or trainings. Good. Very good. Lastly, Alexander pulled up a map of the neighborhood so he could plan out how he was going to scope the house. Their house sat in the middle of a cul-de-sac. What is it with all these families living in a cul-de-sac house? Their street connected to a run through between two main roads. The park where he first saw the children was only five minutes or so down the road. This street wouldn't work the best for running around the neighborhood without people taking notice. Any runners would congregate at the park trails to get their run in versus trying to run where cars were guaranteed to zoom through trying to get to the other main road. That's ok. It wouldn't be the first time that he'd run into this problem. He always had a ready-made story for the occasion should anyone take notice of him and come up to chat like most nosy neighbors are bound to do in the South. He zoomed in on the houses surrounding the family's home to get their numbers and began the same type of search for those neighbors that he ran on the family. Part of power is knowledge, and if he could clue in on the neighbor's schedule, he could find the best time to canvas the street with the least amount of exposure.

But first, a shower and some food.

23

Alexander found that the family's neighborhood was the most quiet between noon and three p.m. over the next few weeks. Most of the street left for work in the morning and didn't come back until that evening like most of the working-class America. This time also allowed stay-at-home parents the opportunity to run errands before they waited in the car rider line at the kids' school, or in enough time to make it home before the bus route dropped off their kid. It's also the time where he could leave his car at the park and then complete his run from the park to the family's cul-de-sac and back without being noticed. Once he deviated from this timeframe and one of the older ladies up the road was out watering her plants. She waved at him and he waved back. He made his way to the cul-de-sac and pretended to catch a cramp in front of the house just before the Wallace's. He noted the camera doorbell on the Wallace's front door, but did not see any other camera within his purview.

Once he passed by her house after his turnaround, she made sure she was checking her mailbox as he passed, just like the busybody Alexander knew she was. She introduced herself and politely asked him if he was new to the neighborhood because she hadn't seen him before. He lied and stated that he had recently bought a house not far from the neighborhood. She told him about the park close by and asked if he'd checked it out yet for his runs, since that's where most people went. He'd told her that he'd checked it out, but the park wasn't big enough for the length he needed since he was training for a marathon, so he ran into the neighborhood and back. Alexander made sure he didn't stop bouncing while they talked to subtly suggest that this didn't need to be a long conversation and that he really needed to get back to running. She nodded in understanding. She mentioned that her son also liked to do marathons in his free time and that he had just finished some sort of fun run for his office to raise money for some sort of charity. Alexander pretended to pay attention, but the words left his head as soon as they left her mouth. Alexander gave the obligatory lie with enthusiasm about how great it was that her son participated in runs for charity and invited her to let him know if another opportunity arose. Her smile widened and she promised to do so. With her questions answered and her wrong assumption that he wasn't a bad fellow intact, she allowed him to resume his run. He put his headphones back into his ears and attempted to find his pace again.

--—

Ten days after his deviation he made his way through the Wallace's backyard. He was surprised to find one of those farm fences surrounding the backyard versus a privacy fence. Seems the Wallace family cares more about the appearance of security, based on the fence and the doorbell without actually focusing on security since that appeared to be the only measures they took with the house. He pulled his gloves from his pocket and put them on as he walked up to the back door. Not even a deadbolt. So easy to get in if someone wanted to. He picked the lock and made his way through the threshold.

He gazed into the living room. To the right sat a TV on top of some trendy farmhouse entertainment center that would inevitably be replaced when the next big home décor fad came around. Besides, it's not like they spent an arm and a leg on it. Alexander examined the build of it. It was obviously a DIY job the wife asked the husband to manufacture on one of his days off, and he had absolutely no skill. Alexander murmured to himself that Mr. Wallace should keep his day job. The TV looked like one husbands dream about for their Sunday football parties. Compensation of the DIY job no doubt. Across from the TV sat a U-shaped couch with a coffee table in front of it. He noted that in case he needed to lay low for a moment when he came next, in the scenario someone needed a midnight snack or the dad needed to check the door locks again to make sure they were locked or else he couldn't sleep. The kitchen was just behind the couch through a doorway. He continued his walkthrough. The front door was just past the living room. To the left a dining room. To the right a long entrance way. What a weird house. He walked to the front door and checked the locks. Just a regular deadbolt and doorknob, unlike the Jones family. He'd need to remember to bring his little wedge for the bottom of the door in case someone managed to run and get the door unlocked.

Alexander turned and went down the long hallway. The first door on the left opened up into a hallway closet. The door directly across, just behind the TV wall, led to a bathroom. Next to the bathroom were both of the children's bedrooms. He opened up the first door, the one next to the bathroom. The teal wall paint made his eyes hurt immediately. Who lets their kid have a room this bright? He turned his attention to the window in the room. The daughter's desk faced it so she could look out the window while she did her homework. Alexander unlocked the window and it slid up easily. A chirp sounded. So, a little more security than he originally thought. These kids hadn't figured out how to disable them yet. Or at least little sister hadn't. He thought back to Sophie, and a smile tipped up the corner of his mouth. She was much more interesting than all the others. She put up a challenge. He slid the window back down and left the room.

Next came the son's room. He opened the cracked door and came face-to-face with a home office. A home office? Where does the son sleep? He turned around and opened the door across the way. Clearly, this was the master bedroom. He counted the doors of the hallway again and scratched his eyebrow. The son lives in the house. He has to. He's seventeen and still in high school. He pulled out his phone and pulled up the house plans. A basement! A basement?

They let their seventeen-year-old sleep in a basement? Did he miss the door? He went back down the hallway and into the living room. He checked his watch. He couldn't remember just how much time he had left to get through the home, but that's why he set the timer on his phone. His eyes darted to each wall and caught sight of a doorknob near the entertainment center. He would loop back to the parents' bedroom. The family didn't have any registered firearms, but this was Georgia. A lot of folks kept their gun collection under wraps, no matter how they voted.

He opened the door and was met with the kind of dark staircase that most little children would find scary, imagining monsters waiting in the edges of the blackness. If only kids knew that the only kind of monster lurking in the shadows had with human faces. He found the light switch to his right and turned it on. He walked down the stairs, noting any creaks he might contend with later. He found one on the bottom step. He would need to remember that a few days from now. Off the stairs he saw a den designed for kids. Another entertainment center. A smaller TV, probably moved from the living room when the other was purchased. The shelves next to the TV held various DVDs and gaming consoles. Everything teenagers needed to waste away their days when not in school. They must be the hang out house for the kids' friends and neighbors. His grandmother never would have allowed his attendance here. Too much temptation for sin and the games too violent. She might not have cared about him enough to supervise him properly between her church activities, daytime soaps, and bingo, but she cared about the perception of her little boy. She would be damned if her grandson was seen playing violent games and watching godless movies filled with sinful sex with all the other children whose families attended church with her on Sundays. In her mind, she was raising a boy who needed to be better than the others because he already had his parents' sins as strikes against him. It didn't matter that everyone avoided him and that nobody wanted to be his friend anyway. She saw it just as much as Alexander did growing up. Adults were nice enough, but he was labeled the "strange" boy, no doubt due to his druggy mother abandoning him, they often said in whispers. After he beat up Eddy Garner in the seventh grade and broke his arm, kids either outright avoided him or pretended to be nice like the adults when they were forced to interact with him. Alexander treated them all the same. He preferred to be alone. Alone with his computer where he practiced all his skills. His grandmother hired the local "computer genius" to put up all the different firewalls and child blocks that computers had at that time when she finally agreed to get him one for his fifteenth birthday. They didn't last long, not that his grandmother would have been able to tell.

Alexander scanned the area. He noticed a cracked door off to the side. He walked over and opened the door. So, this is where the boy slept. That's a lot of trust from the parents to give the boy his own space like this. They probably got tired of his late-night teenager tendencies and agreed to give him the downstairs room on the condition that he went to bed timely and kept his grades up. Or maybe they just figured he'd be going to college next year... *or was*... and so he could be allotted more independence. He examined the room just as he did the sister's. Nothing exciting. Normal teenage boy stuff that he'd found in each room before. The warning timer went off on his watch as he made his way back up the stairs to check out the parents' room.

He made quick work of going through the nightstands. Other than some interesting toys that kids would be mortified to know existed in the drawers, the parents kept just knick-knacks next to the bed. Nothing to defend themselves. Alexander smiled. He always found these trusting types interesting. How can they live in this day and age, in the South no less, without having something to defend their home from an intruder? Every other home did. Their bullets normally are kept separate from the guns because of kids, but at least they had a gun in case of emergency. He scanned the bedroom one more time. A thought struck him, and he dropped to his knees and lowered himself onto his belly. Nothing but luggage under the bed. He decided to run his hands under the mattress on each side just in case. His fingers grazed something hard and cold. He gripped the object and pulled it out. A little .38 special. Now this made more sense. A little gun to make you feel safe below the bible belt. He opened the cylinder and saw a round in each chamber.

"I underestimated you, Mr. Wallace," he chuckled.

He tilted the gun and the bullets dropped into his open palm. He won't notice they're gone unless he's the type to check the bullets before bed. The chances of that are slim so he'll take those odds. Besides, if he did check it, he would likely assume one of his kids or his wife messed with it, and would set a mental reminder to talk to his kids in the morning once his wife denied knowledge of what happened to the bullets. Alexander's watch beeped with the "get out of there" alarm. He'd stayed the maximum amount of time he allotted himself. *Time to go.* He put the gun back where he found it and made a quick swipe on the wife's side just in case. No gun. He made his way back through the house and out the door. He popped off his gloves and stuffed them into his pocket. Once inside his car, he picked up a burner phone he'd gotten from the Walmart two towns over and dialed the three digits he needed.

"911. What's your emergency?"

"Help! There is someone in my house! I think he has a gun! Someone needs to get here now!" Fake panic laced his voice. The operator asked for the address, and he provided the address for the house two doors down per usual. "Oh my God! He's coming!" He ended the call with a click.

He noted the time on the dash and waited. Thirteen minutes later, a police car sped past him with blaring sirens. Not enough time to get in and get out. He noted the time in his journal. He clapped it closed and headed back to the motel. He had a few more days of planning and surveillance ahead of him, so he would take the rest of the afternoon off to relax. He might check out the diner he passed by earlier. Their sign said best burger in the county, so he thought he should test their claim.

24

Officer Danner looked over at his partner while he put the car into drive. He flicked on the flashing blue lights, checking to make sure the coast was clear before pulling out into on-coming traffic. His partner already had the address pulled up in the system. The little car on the GPS turned onto the course and followed the blue line like Dorothy with the stupid brick road.

"You know I don't need that, Rookie. I know where I'm going. That nosey lady who calls us at least once a week lives down that way."

Officer Epsen looked at the address. "Oh yeah... I just have her address memorized at this point, so when it wasn't the same house number I just put the address in without thinking. But even though we know where we're going, it'll help with finding the house quickly."

"It's in the cul-de-sac. What did I say about learning your neighborhoods and where you're going? It will serve you well."

They sped down the roads and turned into the street by the park. "Ok, Rookie, we need to keep our eyes open since this is a break-in call by an unidentified male. Remember what the captain said. Look for any cars parked around here. If you see one, look to see if there is someone in the car."

"Even though we'll be speeding past on our way to what may possibly be a real emergency?"

Danner cut his eyes to his partner. "Epsen, if you're going to be a good cop, you need to be able to notice, identify, and assess a situation within seconds. There is no time for panic or other thoughts. Get your head in the game, because this guy could be targeting our area again. And I'll be damned if we could have done something to stop him but we didn't because of you."

"What do you think the odds of that are, Danner? I mean, he's already hit us once with what, the first murder, wasn't it? What are the chances he's coming back to our part of the state?"

"I'd say pretty fucking high since he just hit her partner's town twice in a row. Why wouldn't he circle back around to Burn's town?" Danner growled in a way that indicated Epsen better not continue questioning him.

Epsen nodded his head and turned his attention to his side of the road while they drove toward their destination.

They reached the house and pulled up into the driveway. The garage door was down and the driveway was empty. They got out of the car and pulled their guns from the holsters before splitting to opposite sides of the house. Epsen checked the front door and found it locked. He checked each window and found the same. He walked around the home and met up with Danner. Danner asked Epsen if he'd found anything, and Epsen shook his head to the contrary. Danner reached the last door around back and attempted to open it. No luck. They looked at each other.

"Well, we can't tell if there is a car in the garage because there are no windows on the garage door."

They stood at the door and listened for any noise that might identify anyone inside. Nothing. They agreed to check around the home again as well as all the doors and windows, just in case they missed anything. Both reached the same conclusion. They got back into their car and Danner radioed into dispatch.

"Dispatch, repeat the address for me please."

Dispatch repeated the location.

"Dispatch, there is no one here as far as we can tell. This appears to be a false alarm."

A silver Cadillac Escalade pulled up to the left of them in the driveway. A woman got out of the car. Fear and confusion covered her face. Danner advised dispatch to standby due to someone pulling up and got out of the car to greet the woman. They introduced themselves and asked if she was the woman who lived at this residence. The woman advised that she lived here with her family. They asked for her name and then advised her of the 911 call they received. She stood confused, and let the officers know that her children were in school, and that her husband would be out until late showing houses. Epsen once again politely asked her to identify herself.

"Beverly White," she stuttered out, her fingers running across her string of pearls to self-soothe some of her trembling. Danner asked the woman if she wouldn't mind them walking through the home to ensure that there were no concerns before heading out. The woman shook her head in agreement and went back into her car to press her garage door opener. They waited for the door to rise before following her in the garage. By that time, Mrs. White had pulled up the app on her phone that displayed where everyone's phone was, then sighed in relief. She pointed the screen in their direction and both officers examined the locations. No other phone for the family showed anyone at the location. They advised that they would still like to take a look around, just to be absolutely safe before leaving her alone in the residence. They followed her into the home and searched the rooms. Once they determined with certainty that Mrs. White could safely be left alone, they thanked her for her time and cooperation and apologized for any inconvenience. Mrs. White, no longer shaking at this point, thanked them for their time and vigilance and led them out of the door and through the garage. Danner got into the car and Epsen opened his car door before he turned back toward Mrs. White.

"Ma'am? I need to ask you one more question before we leave." Mrs. Wallace perked up in response. "Ma'am, who all lives in your home with you? You said your family, but how many live in the home?"

"Oh, just me, my husband, and my kids. You saw the names on the app when I showed you where each one was located."

"I understand that ma'am. I just wanted to be sure. So it's just the four of you? Two kids?"

Confusion with a touch of annoyance creeped into her answer. "Yes, why?"

"An older boy and a younger daughter perhaps?"

Annoyance filled her mouth and she glared at him. "No, a younger son and older daughter. What does it matter, Officer?"

Epsen went to answer but Danner's voice cut him off as his raised voice blared from inside the car. "Thank you for your time, ma'am!" His lowered voice ordered Epsen to get into the car and shut up.

"Don't freak her out," he said through gritted teeth. "All we have is a possibility. We have to call this in and let the captain know what we found. The rest is up to Detective Burns to decide since she's the expert on this guy. Now... radio what we found and call the captain right after." Danner backed out of the driveway while Epsen did as ordered.

"Danner, look out for a four-door silver car parked on your side of the street now that we're leaving. It's the only car I saw on our way in with a driver in the car," Epsen noted.

"Roger that."

25

Angela's cell phone vibrated on the table. She turned from the board and picked it up. The captain's voice rang out so loud she pulled the phone away from her ear. She put it on speaker and then laid it on the table.

"Birdie from dispatch emailed you a recording they got earlier today. According to her, Danner and Epsen went out and it was a bust, so I need you to listen to it and verify if it's William calling in. Danner and Epsen have been instructed to document everything right now until you verify the voice. If it's him, you and Tad need to come in and talk to them. After that, we'll need to find out who lives in the neighborhood."

Tad chimed in. "Angela and I determined based on house numbers and Internet maps that each call was two houses down from the intended victims, so we only need to look at the neighbors two houses to the left and right."

"Copy that. I expect a call back within the next few minutes with verification." With that, he hung up the phone.

"I hate it when he doesn't say goodbye," huffed Angela. "He only does that to get under my skin."

Tad raised an eyebrow at her. "Really? That's high on your pet peeve list? Someone not saying goodbye on the phone?"

She glared at him. "You grow up with my mother and with her deep need to instill Southern lady etiquette, despite my father's eye rolls, and tell me if not saying goodbye wouldn't come across as rude and ill-mannered to you too."

He held up his hands in surrender. "Fair enough. Now let's listen to this call."

Angela drug her finger back and forth along the touchpad to bring her screen up and she unlocked the computer. Her email pulled up after some lag and she waited until the inboxed refreshed. She clicked on Birdie's email and hit play on the recording. Alexander's voice filled the room pretending to be scared, demanding that the police come right away. Angela and Tad turned to face each other with a smile. She redialed the captain's number.

"We got him."

Angela and Tad arrived at the precinct and walked into the conference room where Danner and Epsen sat waiting. Tad noted that they barely made eye contact with Angela as they nodded toward her in greeting. They shook Tad's hand and each met his gaze. Angela warned him in the beginning that everyone from her department avoided her aside from the captain, but this example shown down on him like a spotlight. She said she understood... that they had families to protect and that everyone who got close to her had a target on their back. Tad knew just how true that was with the threat of what this killer wanted to do to him weighing on his shoulders. That still didn't stop him from wanting to punch each man for their cowardice and lack of solidarity to another officer. Instead he clenched his jaw and sat down across from them, quiet.

Angela ran the discussion with the two uniforms. He kept his eyes trained on the men while Angela advised them to start from the beginning. Danner and Epsen took them through the series of events and then stated that the family didn't match the family type of the previous victims. Tad almost responded that the beforehand 911 calls weren't the intended victims, but shut his mouth when he felt Angela's hand squeeze his leg under the table. She didn't want this information getting out, even to other cops. She asked if they noted anything else during their response. Epsen stated that upon arrival, there was a silver four-door sedan parked along the road. He believed it to be occupied but wasn't completely confident in the observation due to the speed in which they drove through the neighborhood to get to the house. Angela asked about body-cam or dashboard footage in the cruiser. Epsen and Danner looked at each other without saying anything. *Of course they hadn't thought about body cam footage or the dash cam.* Angela had to stop herself from rubbing her eyes in frustration. She requested both sets of footage by the end of the day so they could find out if anything else could be identified from the car in question. Two leads in one day was too good to be true after two years of nothing but dead bodies and taunts. She then thanked the officers for their time and assistance. Epsen nodded his head and left from the room as quickly as he could manage without trying to look too eager to get as far away from Angela as he could. Danner walked to the doorway but hesitated. He turned back around and thought for a moment before speaking. Angela and Tad waited for whatever would come out of his mouth. He locked eyes with Tad first.

"Detective, I wanted to say how sorry I am for the loss of your partner. From what I hear, he was also your best friend. I can't imagine, and I'm sorry." He turned his attention toward Angela and met her gaze for the first time since they entered the room. "I hope we were able to help, and I hope you get this son of a bitch...and I don't mean just catch him."

Angela and Tad both acknowledged his words with a nod, and Danner left to follow Epsen back to their desks.

"Danner?" Tad asked. Angela shook her head in confirmation. "Danner said what we're all thinking. We're not hoping you catch him. We're hoping you get him."

She locked eyes with Tad and sighed. "No. You know as well as I do that that's not the job. The job is to bring this guy to justice, not to kill him. Not if I have a choice."

They both thought silently how they knew he wouldn't give her a choice.

Within the hour, Danner and Epsen sent their cam footage to Tad and Angela. In the email, they stated that they didn't see anything on there showing the car aside from a quick flash. Angela pulled up the footage scene by scene. They were right. Nothing but a quick flash. She saw a figure in the car, but the tinted windows disrupted any details they could obtain. The video didn't capture the license plate. She held her hands together over her lips, almost like in prayer, to calm her breathing. Even though she knew it was too good to be true to get more than one lead, she couldn't help feeling like she was going to crawl out of her skin. She'd never been this close before, yet so far away. It felt like agony.

After that they went through the footage, they pulled up the address from the call as well as the addresses from two doors down on either side. If neither address produced the type of family they were looking for, they would branch out. Tad took the house two doors to the left and Angela to the right.

"Would it be bad form to make a wager on which one of us is going to pick the house with the next family?"

Before Angela could answer, Captain Armstrong spoke up from behind them in the doorway. "Yes, but sometimes we have to do things in bad form within the confines of our precinct to keep our sanity. My money is on Angela." He gave her a wink and she smiled.

"You always bet on me."

"Because I know you always win." The smile dropped from his face. "Anything from the footage?"

"It was too much to hope for, sir," Tad answered.

"Need any help with the family lookups?"

"Nope. We may if neither address pans out though," Angela said.

"I'll be in my office if you need me, but just keep me updated. If we find the family today, we need to come up with a plan for their safety ASAP."

Tad and Angela both acknowledged the captain before turning back to their screens. Ten minutes later, Angela popped her head up from the screen and announced her victory.

"Yahtzee!"

"Yahtzee? How old are you that you said Yahtzee to announce your win?" Tad's face crinkled as if he had suddenly smelled a foul odor.

Angela smirked at him. "If you don't like what I say then you can find yourself another partner and another case like you should have done in the beginning."

He smiled that high-wattage smile she loved so much. "Then who would talk to me so sweetly and appreciate me like you do?"

"I'm going to ignore that," but the smile she tried to hide on her face gave her away. "Anyway, so the family two doors down on the right are the Wallaces. Parents are Matthew and Diane Wallace. Older son, Peter Wallace: age seventeen. Younger daughter, Hadley Wallace: age fourteen. Dad is in real estate. Mom works at some accounting firm as a secretary. What do you got?"

Tad shook his head. "Nothing that matches. The parents are separated. Mom and the children are currently in the home based on what I saw, but dad is staying with his girlfriend according to social media. They have two kids but they're both boys."

Tad and Angela took the information over to the captain. Captain Armstrong told them that the family would need to be picked up today now that they have been identified, in case Alexander escalated his timetable. The plan needed to be discreet though, just in case he was watching the family. The captain called Epsen and Danner into his office.

"Go back to the neighborhood and pretend to go door-to-door checking with the neighbors, asking if they've 'seen anything out of the ordinary.' Advise them that a 911 call was received and that y'all are just doing your due diligence even though it appeared to be a false alarm. Keep it vague. Keep it casual. Don't alarm anyone. When you get to the house two doors down to the right of the house—"

"To the right if you're looking at the house or if you were in house, sir?" asked Danner.

"To the right if you're looking at the house," Angela answered.

"When you get to the house two doors down to the right, check to make sure that they are the Wallace family. Tell them to pretend that nothing is wrong, but that they need to pack up a few nights of clothing and get out of the home. Do not notify anyone. If anyone asks, one of them received a call from their mother or something that they fell and they needed to go be with the parent who is at the hospital. Or some other story that would make sense why they packed their bags and left so quickly."

"Wouldn't it be better if Detective Burns went door-to-door with us and was the one who spoke to the family? Or Detective Wilson?"

"If he's stalking these people and he sees Burns or Wilson, he's going to be tipped off that we're onto him. It's public knowledge that they are the only detectives on this case and they're working solely on this case. Burns and Wilson will debrief the family once they get to the station. Now, as I was saying, they need to pack their bags and leave the home. They will then come to the precinct, where we will take their car to the impound lot so it won't be seen in the parking lot, which I don't have to tell you will also tip off this guy. Are we understood?"

Epsen and Danner expressed their understanding and left to complete their assignment.

The captain turned his attention to Angela and Tad. "Once you debrief the family, we'll move them to a hotel outside the county. You two will not be transporting them. I will assign different officers to that task that way maybe we can get them to safety. You two are also to take the family's car from the impound lot tomorrow and drive it back to the home to make it appear as if the family is still there. You two will stake out the home since pattern says he strikes within days of the response time call."

Angela and Tad nodded their understanding and went back to the conference room. Tad sat across from Angela and watched her sit in the chair, unmoving for a few minutes. If he hadn't been paying so close attention, he would have missed the slight tremble in her hands. Her nostrils flared with each breath out as she attempted to steady her breathing. He guessed her heart sounded like a hummingbird's right about now. He stopped himself from getting out of his chair, getting on his knees in front of her, and taking her hands in his to help ground her to this place. Instead, he touched his foot to hers under the table.

"Look at me, Angela."

She ignored him. He tapped her foot harder this time.

"Angela, look at me."

Her eyes met his, but she didn't see him.

"Focus on me, Angela. If you don't focus on me, I will be forced to out us to God and everyone in this precinct. I will come across this table and kiss you back into the present."

Her attention finally focused on him. She glowered at him. "That's not a thing, you know. Kissing someone back to the present. That's not a thing."

"No? Because it seems to me that the very threat of me kissing you is enough to bring you back to the present." He didn't smirk like he normally would. He was still examining her body language to gauge her anxiety.

Her thumbnail rubbed back and forth over her lips. "I'm so close. I've never been this close. All of this is so close to being over. I'm finally going to catch William." She caught herself and corrected her mistake. "We. We are going to catch him."

He smiled but it didn't reach his eyes. "Nice of you to finally accept the 'we.' I half expected you to try and get me to sit out the final take down."

"No, you deserve to be there, even though I don't want something to happen to you. I couldn't have done this without you, and you deserve to bring him in for what he did to your family."

They stared at each other in silence for a few moments and resumed their work, preparing for what was ahead.

———

Alexander sat in the middle booth of the corner diner waiting on his cheeseburger and side salad. He placed his headphones in his ears after he made the order so that the waitress didn't feel the need to try and rope him into a conversation like most diner waitresses did in these type of establishments, especially since it was after the lunch rush and there wasn't a line of people waiting to sit once a booth became available. She could take the time to talk to him if he was inclined. She once asked him what he was listening to, and he replied that it was a true crime podcast. She looked the type that read dime store romances where the men with long flowing hair held some angelic-looking woman on the cover, one who couldn't even watch the news, let alone fill her ears with some dark and twisted crime that happened years ago. Her tight smile and small nod while refilling his water cup confirmed his suspicions. She didn't try to talk to him anymore. Nothing actually played from his headphones. He liked being able to listen to conversations without people being concerned that he was listening in. People spoke more freely when they thought the person closest to them couldn't hear them. As it happened, two cops sat in the booth behind him talking about things they'd seen that day so far in their shift.

"You hear Epsen and Danner might have caught one of those calls the captain warned us about? They supposedly responded to a burglary call or something, and then I saw them later meeting with Burns and that other detective... I can't remember his name."

"Yeah, I saw that too. After the meeting, Epsen and Danner left to go back out. I asked Nancy if she knew anything. You know she hears everything, being the secretary and all."

"Not including her being the biggest gossip in the place," the officer sitting right behind him chuckled.

"She didn't know anything. I'm hoping they found something and this psycho can finally be put away."

"You really think they're going to take him in alive? I figure a guy like that will go out swinging. Not that I care. Personally, I say save the tax payers' money feeding and housing this animal."

"Nah. This sick son of a bitch is going to want his glory. You know serial killers tend to have a fan base."

"You're probably right."

Alexander sipped his coffee as he listened to the officer's chatter. *Did baby sister finally catch up to him?* He resisted the smile threatening to expose him. His thumb rubbed across his lips. Was this the moment he'd been waiting for?

He'd have to change his whole plan. A bolt of excitement hit him. He picked up his cell phone sitting face down on the table. It might be too early, or Mr. Wallace might forget to update his calendar if they're onto him, but it couldn't hurt to check. He unlocked his phone and opened the calendar app he had attached to Mr. Wallace's account. Lo and behold the previous calendar appointments were gone. This time, Alexander allowed himself to smile.

"You got yourself a nice smile there, hon," the waitress said as she poured another round of coffee in his mug.

"I just got some good news actually," he flicked his eyes to her before returning to his phone screen.

"Well, congrats on whatever it is," she smiled at him.

"Thank you, ma'am. Can I get the check please? Also, I would actually like to pay for the officers behind me's meal if I may."

"Oh well honey, that's so sweet! Of course you can." She pulled out her pad and ripped off two receipts. "You just pay over at the register when you're ready, hon."

If she calls me hon one more time, I'm going to take this knife and stab her in the neck.

She must have seen the thought cross his face because her smile dropped, and she abruptly turned around as fast as she could while attempting to remain polite.

I let my face slip.

He drained his coffee and got up from the table. He stopped next to the officers' table. He plastered on the disarming smile he'd practiced throughout his life once again.

"Excuse me, officers. I didn't mean to eavesdrop on your conversation, but by chance are you two talking about that guy killing families?" The officers nodded. "I just wanted to say that I agree with y'all that I think he wants the fame and glory and all that other stuff that comes along with being an infamous serial killer." Alexander watched the officers exchange a look that said they'd said too much in public. "But I don't want to take up any of you guys' time. I just wanted to say I agree, and thank y'all for all that y'all do. Lunch is on me." He watched relief wash over the officers. The officers thanked him and Alexander just nodded in response before going to the register and paying for both meals. A total of thirty-seven dollars seemed worth the invaluable information he had just obtained. Alexander got into his car and opened the glove compartment to grab a burner phone. He turned it on and punched in the number for Mr. Wallace. He picked up on the third ring.

"Mr. Wallace, I got your card from a friend of mine, and I was wondering if I could enlist you in procuring a home. If you're available, that is."

Alexander heard rustling in the background and Mr. Wallace sounded a bit out of breath. "Umm... my apologies, but I actually had a family emergency come up and I'll be out of the office for at least a couple of days. I can let you know when I'm back in the office, or if you don't want to wait, I can recommend a few co-workers who can assist you."

"Oh no, that's ok. I can wait until you're back in the office. I'll just give you a call next week and we'll talk."

"Sounds good. Have a good day." Alexander heard the phone click on the other end and a smile lit up his face, but not one he liked to show in public. This one sent shivers down spines and goosebumps to forearms. He made a mental note to go by the house just to confirm his suspicions. It would take time to get the family somewhere hidden and to get Angela and the other one to set up the house as a trap. He didn't expect more officers to be joining them. Little sister would wait as long as it took, he was sure. They had that in common. He tossed the burner out of the car window and then headed back to the hotel.

Once he reached the motel, he pulled out his father's journal from the bottom of the pile. A green sticky note marked a journal entry about a fourth of the way into the pages. He opened the composition notebook and read his father's words. He scribbled different ways Angela could die, but this one was Alexander's favorite. This was the one that had pushed his father over the edge and into therapy. This one was the one he imagined his would-have-been stepmother reading when she found his secret hidden within the office desk drawer. His ran his fingertips over his father's words. He didn't need to read the scrawl on the page. He committed this entry to memory years ago when he found his sister and planned out this game they played. He didn't know how long all of this would last when it first began, but he always knew this was how it would end. He pictured his sister's blue eyes looking up at him as they dimmed into lifelessness. A tingle ran up his spine at the thought. He imagined for a moment about what would happen next after he killed Angela, but quickly pushed that question out of his mind. He didn't want to think about how nothing might excite him quite like this in the future. It didn't matter now. His future self would find something else to excite him. Maybe he'd start making snuff films. His nose crinkled and his mouth fell into a frown. Barbaric. No, he didn't believe snuff films would be his next venture. He cleared his mind and pulled out his personal journal to get started on the plan ahead of him.

26

Angela sat her service weapon on the coffee table in front of her. She and Tad spent the last two days familiarizing themselves with the home and the grounds. Even though the both of them knew William's pattern told them he wouldn't strike until tonight, they still prepared in case his plans changed. They placed small alarms on each locked window and door so the chances of William surprising them greatly lessened. Each hour they took turns patrolling outside the house and calling it in to the captain.

Angela found this neighborhood much like hers, quaint and quiet. The kind of neighborhood that most families want their children to grow up in. That's why she bought her house years ago. Back when she believed she would someday have a family to raise. Her eyes drifted to the window when she saw Tad's figure pass in front of it as he walked around the house. She wouldn't have minded having a family with him. She knew he wanted one. Before Nick and June were murdered, they often joked with Tad that he needed to hurry up and find his wife and make babies, because their kids weren't getting any younger and needed cousins around. Angela and Tad had never discussed the future. She refused to, considering that she wasn't sure she would survive the inevitable battle with her brother. Tad just always held her in his arms while they lay in bed, saying they would have time after all this was over. He believed in her. Angela wasn't so sure.

"No news is good news," Tad declared, dragging her out of her own thoughts when he came back in through the back door.

She smiled weakly in response. She picked up her gun and undid her mag. She'd checked her gun at least a dozen times. Same with the one strapped to her ankle. She kept checking her bullet supply to make sure she wouldn't be in short supply if she needed them.

"It's probably too early anyway. Most of the 911 calls were well after midnight."

Tad sat down next to her. He wanted to grab her hand or do something to show his support, but he knew now wasn't the time. He glanced at his watch. 10:02. He figured like she did that they had a few hours left to wait. The captain had a tactical team on standby if they didn't check in every hour. They all agreed that Angela and Tad could handle themselves until back up arrived, and that having too many people around the home or street would tip him off. Angela believed her brother already knew. She couldn't explain her reasoning. She just knew that he knew. Tad tried to convince her that there was no way that he could know. She just looked at him and explained it was just that kind of underestimating that would get him killed if he didn't watch it. He almost snapped back when she said that to him, but he reminded himself that she knew better than him, and that he somehow got the drop on Nick, who was always prepared to defend his family. He got up from the couch for a glass of water and asked Angela if she needed anything from the kitchen. She declined. She hadn't eaten or drank all day, despite Tad reminding her that she needed to eat and drink water to keep up her strength. She just shook her head and said she didn't think she could keep anything down. She was more than wired. Keeping up her strength wouldn't be an issue.

———

12:02. Alexander's watch glowed in the darkness. Show time. He'd been watching little sister and Tad take turns outside every hour. For detectives, they really didn't understand hunting. They didn't understand the importance of stillness and surveillance. Tad certainly wasn't stealthy or as on high alert as little sister. He thought for a moment that she almost saw him on her last round. She stared in his direction and waited, watching, but ultimately decided it wasn't him, and continued walking. Between rounds, Alexander crept closer to the far side of the house away from the living room window Angela watched Tad out of each time it was his turn. Tad always went clockwise around the house, starting by the living room and ending where Alexander crouched in the shadows. He really made the job easy. Alexander heard the door open, followed by Tad's footsteps. Alexander clutched the knife in his hand as he waited for Tad to pass by him.

"All clear. Over." The walkie talkie clicked as he let go of the button.

"Copy," answered the captain.

Alexander moved out from the shadows and followed behind. Tad caught the movement and turned toward Alexander. Alexander lifted the knife and brought the handle down to the back of Tad's head. He went down with an audible thump. Alexander twirled the knife in his hand so the tip pointed at Tad, but he lied unconscious on the grass. Alexander turned him onto his back and crouched over him. His hand cupped his jaw and moved it right to left. Tad's head flopped without resistance.

"And they say it's much harder to knock someone out in real life versus the movies," he chuckled to himself. "You made this too easy. But don't worry, once I finish with little sister, I'm coming back for you. You and I are going to have some fun." He resisted the instant, overwhelming urge to slowly insert the knife into his stomach to see if he would wake up. He decided to try it later. After all, he had a schedule to keep. He only had an hour before they had to call it in again, and if they didn't, he figured he had a ten-minute window before every cop in the city showed up with sirens blaring. He didn't think he could convince Angela to call it in even with a knife to her throat, so he had to get moving. He couldn't resist grazing the knife across Tad's cheek.

"You won't like what awaits you, but I will." He smiled.

Alexander grabbed the walkie talkie from Tad's belt and turned it off. He didn't risk throwing it away from Tad or bringing it into the home where Angela could get to it. Turning it off at least bought him a few moments until a disoriented Tad figured out why it wasn't working, if he even woke up before Alexander came back for him. He pulled out Tad's handcuffs and cuffed his wrists together. His hands searched Tad's pockets and belt quickly, but he couldn't find his key for the handcuffs. No matter. As an afterthought, Alexander grabbed Tad's gun from his belt and took out the mag and chambered round. He put the pieces into the bottom pocket of his cargo pants. *No sense in risking being surprised by a bullet.*

Knowing he was safely unconscious, Alexander left Tad on the lawn and headed up the back steps of the house. He opened the door and saw Angela sitting on the couch. She turned her head to say something to Tad, but her eyes widened as she realized who had really just walked through the door. Angela hesitated only a fraction of a second before picking her weapon up and drawing it on him. She told him to freeze. He held up his hands, the knife still cupped in his left hand, as if in surrender. He kicked the door closed and continued to make his way toward her. She stood up and once again told him to freeze.

"Sit back down," he ordered.

"No thanks. I'd rather just cuff you and bring you in. Where is my partner?" Her eyes darted behind him to the back door.

"Don't worry. He's alive outside. He's just not conscious. Now, sit down. Let's chat."

She made no move to sit down.

"You're not going to shoot me. Not in cold blood like this anyway. You're going to try and bring me in like you said. Once you get near me, I'm going to wrestle you for the gun and get it from you anyway, and then make you sit down. So why don't we just save time, shall we? We have a little less than an hour now since I waited until your inept partner out there made the check in call."

Angela kept her gun trained on him but sat back down on the couch. Alexander went into the kitchen and came back with a chair. He placed it on the other side of the coffee table facing Angela.

"I'll put my knife down if you put your gun down," he bargained.

She looked at him like he was speaking a foreign language. "Now why in the world would I do that, William?"

His right eye twitched at the use of his first name. "I don't go by that name, as you well know. And we've already established that you're not going to shoot me, so let us both put down our weapons shall we?"

"I think that's giving me a lot of credit," she said. But she put the gun down in front of her on the coffee table.

He pointed the knife at her. "And now the other one."

She tilted her head, considering whether or not to feign ignorance. She decided against it before leaning down to grab her ankle gun and putting it on the table next to her other one.

Alexander put down the knife in front of him and leaned back in his chair. "So, little sister, are there any questions you're just dying to know since we have some time?"

She studied him. "No, I think I pretty much have you figured out." She watched his nostrils flair and annoyance cross his face before he quickly masked his emotions behind a smile that didn't reach his eyes. Good. She wanted to throw him off his game by not feeding into his belief that he was some grand mastermind.

"Enlighten me," the words melted out of his mouth. His head tilted to the side and his unblinking eyes stayed fixed on her face. He reminded her of a viper staying trained on a target before striking.

"I think your feelings on our father are clear. You don't go by the name you share with him and you gut each father like a fish each time you kill a family."

"I'm sure over these past few years you've done your research on our father, and I hope the two gifts I left you in your mailbox helped. Was he really a man someone should strive to be?"

She ignored his question. "And yet for someone you find so gutless, you sure have a lot of anger toward the man. You stabbed each father a multitude of times after cutting him open."

This time he ignored her.

"You go by your middle name, Alexander. 'A' in your notes to me. You take it easy on the brother for obvious reasons. You even go easy on these mothers. That tells me as angry as you are toward your own mother, you have compassion for her, which strikes me as odd considering you're a sociopath."

"Or maybe I just don't have enough time, and I focus on the two most important ones."

"No, that's not it. You don't call 911 until after the families are dead, so technically you could take all the time you wanted. With the exception of Brooklyn of course. You wanted to ensure she was alive when I got there so I could watch her suffer with those words carved into her torso before she died."

"Ah yes, little eleven-year-old Brooklyn. How does it feel to know that little girl suffered so much because of you? That all of them suffered because of you? Did she ever regain consciousness before she died? Don't answer that. According to your local reporter, I know she didn't. And she tends to get the story right. What's her name? Casey something... I don't know why I can't seem to recall her name right now. I really enjoy reading her stuff. Maybe I'll even let her interview me once I kill you. It'll have to be via telephone of course, since I'll be on the run and all." He leaned in toward her, and a smile broke across his face that sent a cold shiver down Angela's spine. "You know... I'll probably give her my journals after this, that way she has the full story with all the juicy details. I hear she's been wanting to break into true crime novels. I could be her first book. I'll just take my cut straight from her bank account, because I know it'll sell and make her a very wealthy woman. Yes, that's what I will do. I'll spare her no details about how you died, I promise. Our father might not have had the balls to act on his fantasies, but I do. And I plan on bringing one of his to life for him tonight."

He watched fear flash in her eyes before she masked it with anger and laughed.

"Oh, yes, little sister—just like I told your little partner outside—you won't enjoy what happens to you, but I will."

She leaned forward then. Her forearms rested on her knees, challenging him. "All of this just because our father decided to stay with my mother and not yours? All this needless killing when you could have just gone after me in the first place."

He clapped his hands in child-like glee. "Oh, but hasn't it been fun? We never got to play any childhood games as brother and sisters get to do, so I figured we'd make up for lost time. Plus, all of this has made your career. Has it not? You should be thanking me for all of this! You weren't a detective before I came along, and gave you this big case. No one had any clue who you were. Now we are both going to be infamous."

Alexander paused for a moment. "Well...thanking me is probably a bit much considering how this is going to end." He tsked. "You as the loser of course, as all little sisters tend to be. Never outwitting the elder brother."

She took advantage of her position at that moment and reached for one of the guns. Alexander kicked up from under the coffee table and it flipped toward her. Her ankle gun slid under the couch. The other flew against the wall and bounced off to land away out of reach. The table hit her shins. Alexander hurled himself on top of her and reached for her throat.

"What did I just say about not outwitting the older brother?" he said through clenched teeth.

She fought against him and pushed up her hips to buck him off her. He lost his balance and fell to the side. She rolled away from him and crawled toward her gun. He grabbed her ankle and attempted to pull her back toward him. She kicked out with her other leg and heard a curse yell out. She wasn't sure what part of his body she hit, but she didn't care. She found her way to her gun and turned around with her finger on the trigger. She stared at the empty space before her, her breath coming out in pants. She got up off the floor and surveyed her surroundings. He didn't go past her outside and she didn't hear the door of the basement. It was still closed. He had either gone down the hallway to the bedrooms or into the kitchen. The kitchen had two openings to go in and out of, so smart money was on that.

"William... I've had two days to study this house and its layout. You can't hide from me," she called out to him.

He didn't answer.

She kept her gun in front of her as she made her way to the kitchen. "You've been preparing me for this showdown for two years now, and all you're going to do is hide? Is that why you were able to kill those families? Because you hid and got the drop on them like the coward you are?"

She didn't expect the kick from behind. She managed to catch herself just enough to keep a grasp on her gun as she landed on her hands and knees. She turned around and swung her gun wide attempting to connect with his face, but it missed by a whisper. He swung his knife down, but she moved away just enough for it to come down between her legs. She snapped her legs shut and twisted, forcing him to release the knife. She turned the gun to face him. He grabbed her wrist and twisted forcing her to release the gun.

"Turnabout's fair play," he grinned. He aimed the gun at her head and crouched down in front of her. "Now..." he held out his other hand expectantly. "Give me back my knife. Please and thank you."

She released the knife from her thighs, and he picked it up without looking away from her. He stood up and stepped out of reach. He held the knife and gun in one hand while he unloaded her chambered bullet and magazine with the other.

"We don't need this, or these. I don't much care for guns. Don't move now. I'll be right back." He kept the knife pointed at her while he backed up. She watched him open the back door and throw the gun and bullets out into the lawn. He came back to the kitchen. "Now, are you ready for the fun part?"

She didn't answer, but her eyes spoke murder. He answered her with a smile.

"Get up little sister...we're going to go play."

He led her into the bathroom. As they walked, he told her all about how her father used to write down different scenarios of what he wanted to do to her, and how the different ideas were spread out among multiple journals. The journal he'd sent her had some ideas, but he'd kept the journal containing his favorite. He told her about how he'd played with suffocation before, as she's seen, but never drowning. He was saving that one just for her. He wasn't sure if he had the patience but he was willing to try. When they reached the bathroom, she felt the tip of the knife press into her back. He leaned in close and whispered into her ear. He instructed her to turn on the tub and put the stopper down.

She whipped her head towards him. "No."

The knife's tip dug itself further into her back. A slit in the fabric of her shirt was no doubt opening wider and wider as she felt the tip of the knife pierce her skin. Red hot pain lanced in her back. She hissed.

"You can push it all the way into my back and just let me bleed out here. I'm not turning on that water and letting you drown me."

He answered her with a twist of the knife. Her breath left her lungs.

"Go ahead, William. Stab me," she managed to say through gritted teeth.

He grabbed the hair at the base of her skull to keep her still as he leaned forward to turn on the tub himself. As he reached down to plug in the stopper, she twisted her body. She sent her elbow into the crook of his arm to release her hair and shoved his face into the tub spout. She made a run for it.

"You bitch!" she heard behind her.

He tackled her from behind. Her shoulder snapped the overturned table's leg as she went down. He flipped her over and blood from his smashed nose dripped onto her face as he leaned in close.

"You're going to pay for that," he sneered. She bucked and clawed her hands down his face and chest.

Burning pain shot up her body. She felt the knife hilt press against her upper leg.

"You can't run now, little sister." He pulled the knife out and blood poured from the wound.

With one hand wrapped around her throat, he used the hand holding the knife to pull out a large zip tie from the pocket next to his knee. "Normally I use these for restraining people to chairs, but I think I have a better idea for you. I want to see your terror as it tightens around your throat. I want to see the light leave your eyes." His knee moved to her chest to keep her still as he looped the zip tie together. He began to put it over her head.

"No!" She fought against him. She swung her fists at every part she could reach and used her good leg to continue attempting to push him off her body. Her hands finally knocked the knife out of his hands. He leaned to retrieve it and his weight shifted. She used this to her advantage and rolled him underneath her. He grabbed for the knife, but she was faster. She pressed the knife to his chest. He took his thumb and pushed into the wound on her leg. She screamed but did not let go of the knife. His other hand wrapped around her wrist in an attempt to twist the knife from her. She pushed down with all of her might.

His mouth and eyes opened wide in surprise as the knife penetrated his chest. She pulled the knife from his body with a sucking sound. Blood ran down both of his sides. She pushed the knife in again and his eyes met hers.

"No one is going to read your words, William." She leaned in closer. She noticed the blood staining his teeth as his body struggled to suck in air. "I'm going to make sure of that. You aren't going to be infamous. You're just some psycho that people will forget about over time. They won't remember your name."

He tried to answer, but no voice left his lips. She pulled the knife from his body and struck again, forming a third wound in his chest. Blood seeped from the corners of his mouth. His eyes broke from hers to look up at the ceiling. His chest stopped rising and falling underneath her. She grabbed the zip tie intended for her death. She kept the knife pointed at his body as she pushed herself up with her good leg. Her breath heaved and her heartbeat pounded in her ears. Even seeing his body lie still, seeing the blood having stopped flowing when his heart stopped, she didn't believe him to be dead. It couldn't be that easy for the monster she hunted to be put down. She managed to put the zip tie around her thigh and yank, creating a makeshift tourniquet. She didn't turn her back to him as she limped to the back door. Her back hit the wall and she grabbed around for the doorknob. She opened the door and went outside. She didn't turn around until the door shut tightly. She limped as fast as she could down the stairs and searched around for Tad. She found him still unconscious in the grass just outside the house. She tapped his cheek repeatedly, calling his name. He finally roused with a groan.

"Thank God, you're alive!" She sighed. She kissed his lips in celebration.

She picked up the walkie talkie next to him and clicked the button. "Captain! You copy?"

No answer.

"Captain!"

Still nothing. She checked the dials and saw the dial was turned off. She turned the knob and tried again.

"I copy. Over."

She'd never been more grateful to hear that old man's voice in all her life. "It's over. Tad and I need an ambulance." She heard Tad groan that he didn't need one, ensuring that he was fine. Just a little dizzy.

"But we're going to need the coroner for the other guy." Angela grinned at Tad.

"En route. Over."

"Come on, we've got to check his pockets." She managed to pull herself back up off the ground.

"Check his pockets?" Tad asked. He sat up but was pallid, like it was a fifty-fifty shot he was going to pass back out onto the lawn.

"He mentioned having journals. Maybe he'll have some sort of clue in his pockets as to where the rest of them are. Maybe a key, or maybe his address on his license will be correct. I don't know, but we need to check his pockets and do it before anyone else gets here. We've only got a few minutes." She picked the knife back up.

"I thought he was dead since you said coroner." Tad rubbed his head.

"He is, but I'm not taking any chances. Now, are you coming?"

"Of course I'm coming. Just give me a second." He retrieved the key from the inside of his right shoe and uncuffed himself, then looked over at her. "Are you okay?"

"Yeah, I used one of his zip ties to try and stop the bleeding."

Tad just looked at her in confusion.

"He stabbed me. Now let's go. We don't have much time, and I only have one good leg to work with here."

Tad got up from the grass and wrapped his arm around her waist. She threw her arm over his shoulder and he helped her walk back into the house. Angela sat down next to the body with a huff and started to rifle through the pockets. More zip ties. Car key with nothing else on the key ring. She lifted him onto his side and checked the back pockets. Nothing. She laid him back down with a thump.

"Of course it wouldn't be that easy," she mumbled.

"There is a car key. I'm sure any information he might have will be in his car."

"I'm not going to make it to his car, and neither will you. Not in time." She heard the ambulance sirens coming approaching in the distance. "Of course they're already here."

She pocketed the key and waited for everyone to start coming through the door. Captain Armstrong entered in first. He went directly to Angela and looked her over. She told him not to fuss and to come closer. She slipped him the car key and advised that he needed to check the car before any officers or crime scene techs got to it. He nodded as he slipped the key into his pocket. He then wrapped his arm around her waist and pulled her to standing. The EMTs came in through the back door and took over from there. One focused on Angela and helped her get into the back of the ambulance. The other followed Tad, who to no surprise, refused help getting to the other ambulance. He could walk just fine on his own, thank you very much. Before he stepped into the back, he turned to Angela.

"See ya there, honey." He gave her a wink.

She rolled her eyes while laughing. "So dumb," she muttered.

Once she was on the gurney and ready for transport, she reminded the captain to stay behind for now but to come to the hospital later to update her. The captain nodded in confirmation. He watched both ambulances drive away before returning to manage the scene. The medical examiner completed his work and the crime scene technicians took care of the rest. Captain Armstrong couldn't imagine the Wallace's ever living in this house again after tonight. They might come back long enough to move everything out before putting the property up for sale. They might take a loss on it, but maybe Mr. Wallace could work some realtor magic.

After everything was under control, Captain Armstrong left the scene and pushed the emergency button on the car key fob. Nothing happened. He went into his car and drove around pushing the button. Nothing on the family's street. He turned right out of the street and made his way down the road, clicking the button until a car horn finally sounded. He saw the blinking lights on a little Honda car, and he clicked the alarm button again to turn off the noise. He parked in front of the car and unlocked the doors. His gloves went on with a snap on the wrist. He started in the center console looking for something, anything. Nothing. He moved to the passenger side glove compartment. Nothing. He looked under the driver seat and found a black wallet. He opened the wallet and found a license with a fake name. Behind the license, he found a key belonging to a local hotel. He didn't think that William was ever too far from his sister. He was right. He put the wallet back under the seat and locked the car before heading to the hotel.

Thankfully, the room number was on the key so he could bypass announcing his presence to the front desk staff. He snapped on some rubber gloves before touching anything aside from the key. He opened the door to the room and stepped inside. Nothing but clothes in the drawers. He searched the little closet and found a bag in the corner. Inside he found older looking composition books he recognized to match those William had sent to Angela along with newer, leather journals he assumed to be William's. He zipped the bag back up, picked it up, and left the hotel room. Later, he'd give the car key and hotel key to the officers and state that Angela had forgotten that she'd put them into her pocket before leaving the crime scene after she searched the body for a zip tie to tourniquet her leg. Angela and Tad would presumably need some leave due to their injuries, so other officers would assist with evidence gathering in their absence. The case was closed due to William being dead. They just needed to cross the T's and dot the I's at this point. He decided to not risk having the journals in his possession, so he went by Angela's house to drop them off before heading to the hospital. He fed Gizmo too, since he doubted Angela would be home tonight. Gizmo thanked him for his thoughtfulness by cheek rubs to his face.

"She finally did it, Jackson." He looked up at the ceiling. "She's alive and she did it. I know you're proud and I'll tell her so."

27

Tad crouched down in front of his family and placed a bouquet of assorted flowers at both gravestones. He looked at Nick and June's smiling faces in the encapsulated picture and thought back to the conversations they'd had about gravestones. Of course they'd only discussed Nick and June's headstones, never imagining that their kids would be joining them like they did. Nick and June always wanted to share one gravestone. June just assumed Nick would go first and she would join him many years later. Nick always hated that assumption, but June just shrugged her shoulders and reminded him that he worked in a much more dangerous line of work than she did as a housewife. Nick would always kiss her then and tell her that as long as he didn't have to live without her, he didn't care. Tad thought it only right that they buried the kids together and that they shared a headstone like their parents.

"I miss you guys. So much." He scratched his eyebrow and then ran his forefinger and thumb around his lips to steady himself. He came here to talk to them, not cry. Today is not a day for crying. He came here to tell them the news himself even though he was sure they already knew. Even dead, they deserved to hear it from him.

"I'm sorry I didn't come here sooner but I wanted to make sure everything was officially settled first. As you guys know, we got him. We got that son of a bitch. He won't hurt any other family again. Angela made sure of that."

He turned to Nick's name. "You would love her, Nick. She's the badass you always said I needed. She keeps me in line."

He looked at June's name. "June, she's not alone anymore. I know you hated the idea of it when we discussed the case."

He looked over at the kids. "I miss you two knuckleheads."

He turned back to Nick and June. "I broke my lease and am moving to Angela's town. They made my transfer official right after we got him, but Angela and I had to take some time off on account of our injuries and all. Hers took longer to heal than mine since mine was just a concussion but Cap let me use some vacation days that way we could start back to work together. I'll be staying with Angela until I get my own place."

He smirked at Nick's name and imagined Nick's face and him saying, "*If* you get your own place."

"I don't want to leave you guys, but there is nothing left for me here now that you guys are gone. I can't have another partner in this precinct and frankly, Angela's it for me. Both professionally and personally. She feels the same way even though she doesn't want to rush it. I promise next time I'll bring her to say hi. I hope Heaven is awesome."

He sat with them for a little while longer and just talked about nothing in particular.

———

Angela and Captain Armstrong stood in her backyard facing a burn barrel and the stacks of journals. Once the hospital released Angela and Tad, the three of them got to work reading both her father's and her brother's journals. They wanted to make sure the journals didn't connect to any other cases or contain any invaluable evidence. The only portion of one journal Tad skipped contained what happened to Nick, June, and the kids. He said he heard what happened once. He didn't need to hear the details again through the lens of a killer he couldn't bring back to life and murder again. Angela couldn't blame him. All three of them agreed that there was nothing in the journals that weren't the ramblings of mad men or details of the case they didn't already know, aside from William alluding to previous murders he committed. He didn't give those details so Angela and Tad could follow up. He even admitted that he wished he'd started journaling before his game with Angela so he could reread what he did over and over whenever he felt restless. Not to mention it would give a true account of his body count when his journals were published for the world to see.

Captain Armstrong put wood at the bottom of the burn barrel and poured lighter fluid on the wood. He struck a match and threw it into the barrel. He watched the flames rise above the top. "Are you sure Tad doesn't want us to wait?"

"Yeah, he's going to be a while anyway between talking to Nick and June and the kids and his drive time back here. He said this burning was more for me than it is for him anyhow."

The captain nodded. "He's right. How are you feeling about tomorrow?"

"In terms of?"

"In terms of all of it. Tonight Tad will officially be living with you."

"Not that he basically hasn't been living with me for a while between the case and then us reading these journals together during our medical leave."

The captain gave her a look that told her she needed to let him finish. "Tonight, Tad will officially start living with you full time, at least for now. Tomorrow, you two start back at work as partners. You two will be working together, juggling all sorts of cases and not just working one case. It's a lot of change. How are you feeling about it?"

"I was actually going to talk to Tad about him not just staying for now. I know I told him I wanted to take it slow but there is no sense in him leaving if he's just going to move back in at some point anyway. Plus, I know he wants to stay. He's just looking for another place because he wanted to go at my pace. As for work, it looks like I'm no longer going to be ostracized by my peers which I'm pretty excited about. Not that I didn't understand their reasoning, which is what I told every officer who came by during these last few weeks to check on me and bring me and Tad dinner. I'm ready to work on new cases and make a name for myself in a new way...a good way."

"You already made a name for yourself in a good way by catching William."

She returned the look he previously gave her that said, *hold all comments and questions until the end please.* "I'm ready for the next chapter. Pun intended with all these journal entries that we've been reading."

She ripped out the guts of her father's composition books and threw them into the awaiting flames. She watched the pages crumble and finally incinerate. She kept repeating the process until all of her father's words were gone.

"I feel bad for the man. He hated those thoughts and tried hard to rid himself of them. It's sad really. I hope he's at peace now wherever he is."

She moved on to her brother's journals. She couldn't rip them out in one whack like she could her father's pages. Instead, she wrenched out handfuls and chunked them onto the flames with finality.

"Now William can stay dead. His words will never see the light of day and maybe one day he'll just be some forgotten killer among the crowd of killers out there."

His last bits of writing, the ones he wrote for the world, crumbled to ash.

Sometimes there are moments that determine what kind of human you turn out to be. Forks in the road made of choices that lead us one way or another. I knew what kind of human I wanted to

be and what choices I did and didn't want
to make. I wanted to be the person my
father didn't have the guts to become
except for in his writings. I didn't want my
fantasies chained to some lifeless paper. I
needed them to breathe as I watched the
life flicker out of each one of their eyes.
I am not some coward like my father. I am
better. I am a legend. I am infamous.

ABOUT THE AUTHOR

Ann Lowe is someone who has always dreamt of becoming an author. Writing has been a passion for as long as she can remember and she's excited that her dream is finally coming true.

Ann lives in Georgia with her family. She's a full time wife, mom, and social worker. She is a mental health advocate and animal lover. Aside from writing, Ann's hobbies include reading, traveling, indulging in everything true crime, and spending time with the people she loves most.

Made in the USA
Columbia, SC
24 June 2023

485cc7cc-0ece-4bf6-8f27-00c8a40a3ba0R01